D0649691

The
Amazing
Flight of
Darius
Frobisher

Ω
Published by
PEACHTREE PUBLISHERS
1700 Chattahoochee Avenue
Atlanta, Georgia 30318-2112

www.peachtree-online.com

Text © 2006 by Bill Harley
Jacket illustration © 2006 by Michael P. White

An earlier version of this story appeared for a limited time period as an e-book on the website of the Maricopa County Library District under the title of *Flyboy*.

Book design by Loraine M. Joyner
Typesetting by Melanie McMahon Ives

Printed in the United States of America
10 9 8 7 6 5 4 3 2 1
First Edition

Library of Congress Cataloging-in-Publication Data

Harley, Bill, 1954-
    The amazing flight of Darius Frobisher / by Bill Harley. -- 1st ed.
       p. cm.
    Summary: When his adventurous father disappears during a hot-air
balloon flight, ten-year-old Darius is torn away from his beloved
housekeeper and sent to live with an obnoxious aunt until a strange
bicycle repairman with a secret changes his life.
    ISBN 1-56145-381-1
    [1. Orphans--Fiction. 2. Flight--Fiction. 3. Bicycles--Fiction.]
    I. Title.
PZ7.H22655Ama 2006
[Fic]--dc22
                                    2006013993

The
Amazing
Flight of
Darius
Frobisher

by Bill Harley

For the Kidney family—
Dave, Kim, Jenna, and Will, who read it first

Thanks to Jane Murphy who helped bring Darius back to life,
and whose questions made me rethink the whole story.

Thanks to Tim Wadham of the Maricopa County Library District,
who immediately liked what he read. Thanks to the library itself
for their online edition, which made me feel like Charles Dickens.

Thanks to Carmen Agra Deedy
for her faith and encouragement and clear eye and heart.

Thanks to Margaret Quinlin for reading everything.

And thanks especially to my editors,
Emily Whitten and Vicky Holifield, for their care and insight,
and for noticing things I hoped would go unnoticed.

Thanks and love to my wife, Debbie Block,
who has patiently read all the versions.

CONTENTS

We meet Darius

All stories begin somewhere, and this one begins with a large red water balloon sailing through the air toward a black car as it pulled into a driveway.

"Uh, oh," said Darius.

"Oh dear!" exclaimed Miss Hastings, "I didn't see them coming at all."

"Neither did I," said Darius.

The moment he finished his sentence, the water balloon exploded on the front windshield of the car. The tires screeched and the car lurched to a halt. Darius and Miss Hastings watched with some concern from their perch on the roof of the house. They had been shooting water balloons out into the street with a giant slingshot made of rubber tubing. It was Miss Hastings's idea.

Of course, that isn't exactly normal behavior for a housekeeper. But Miss Hastings was trying to cheer Darius up. When you are only eleven years old and your father has disappeared in a hot air balloon, your housekeeper is likely to try anything to lift your spirits.

Especially if she loves you.

Darius peered down at the car. The doors flew open, and two men and a woman hopped out. They were dressed in sleek black, like the car, and they staggered a little as if the water balloon had hit them and not the car.

"You stay here," whispered Darius. "I'll go see who it is."

"I had better come down, too," said Miss Hastings. "They look important."

Darius scrambled back through the third-floor window of the old house and headed to the stairs as Miss Hastings did her best to keep up. Darius scampered downstairs and opened the front door. The woman and two men standing before him still seemed slightly shaken, and their faces looked stern and serious.

Darius had never seen these people before. Since his father had vanished, there had been a lot of adults around him that he didn't know, clucking their tongues and shaking their heads and looking at him with sad eyes. They gave him the creeps. But these three were the worst yet. They reminded Darius of the three gloomy ravens in a song that Miss Hastings often sang to him at bedtime.

But he didn't say this. Instead he was polite and asked, "May I help you?"

"Someone...hit our car...with a water balloon," sputtered the woman, sucking in air as if her breath were trying to get away from her.

"I'm sorry to hear that," said Darius. He decided not to volunteer any more information than necessary. "Are you all right?"

None of them answered. They were busy gasping. After a moment, one of the men caught his breath and said, "Ahem. My name is Figby."

"Yes, ahem," said the second man. He, like the first one, was carrying a shiny black briefcase that matched his suit. "My name is Migby."

"You poor dear," said the woman to Darius. "My name is Katrina Zarnoff. You may call me Aunt Kitty." She reached out and stroked the side of Darius's face. Then without asking, she whisked by him into the house with Figby and Migby close at her heels. They nearly ran over Miss Hastings in the entryway.

"Please, do come in," said Darius. "Since you already have."

Darius thought this was the kind of thing his father might have said to people who entered your house without asking. His father hated pompous people. Darius felt a sharp pang in his heart.

There was something about Darius's father that made him different from other people—and *very* unlike Figby, Migby, and Katrina Zarnoff. (You may call her Aunt Kitty if you like, but Darius isn't going to and neither am I.) Rudy Frobisher was quick to smile and he smiled with his whole face, especially his eyes, which were a very bright blue, like the sky on a clear fall afternoon. This magical smile could raise your spirits even on the dreariest of days. Darius's father lived life boldly, too, which is not something you would expect from an insurance salesman. On the days he wasn't selling insurance to make a living, he went on the most marvelous adventures.

Rudy Frobisher had sailed to Antarctica and stayed with a family of penguins. He had trekked across the steppes of Mongolia and lived on yak's milk. Once, Darius's father had even missed a week of work because he was trapped in a cave filled with thousands of bats and one grizzly bear the size of a mastodon.

Most people thought that Darius's father was crazy, especially when he told them about talking with penguins. But Darius loved hearing every exciting detail of his father's travels. In fact, he loved everything about his dad, even his limp. It was only a small limp, but it caused Mr. Frobisher to pitch slightly to one side as he walked, making his footsteps sound like hiccups. It gave Darius a thrill every time he heard his dad come in the front door. At each uneven step the coins in his dad's pants pocket clinked against his leg, *ching...ching...ching.*

Darius missed his father terribly during his absences, but he knew that his father's travels were part of who he was, like his smile and his limp. In some ways, Mr. Frobisher's time away from Darius and Miss Hastings made him an even better father when he was home. He always came back with the most amazing stories and gifts, and he promised Darius that when he was old enough, he would take him along on an adventure. Even Miss Hastings, who would rather sit on a porcupine than go on an adventure herself, said that Mr. Frobisher always came home relaxed and refreshed.

And he always had come home on schedule, until a few weeks ago. One fine Saturday morning, Darius's father had climbed into a hot air balloon for a weekend jaunt. But he disappeared, as it were, into thin air. The last time anyone saw him, he had been soaring over Newfoundland, headed toward the North Atlantic Ocean on the wings of a great storm. No one knew what happened to him. Not even I know, and I am telling you this story.

And so, the chances seemed high that Darius would never hear the comforting *ching ching ching* of his father's walk again. That prospect was precisely what Figby, Migby, and Zarnoff had come to discuss.

The three visitors sat down on the couch in the living room and opened their briefcases and their mouths. They spoke to Miss Hastings and Darius in a tone of voice that I am sure you have heard before—and that I am sure you hate. It was a tone of voice that said, *We know everything and you are idiots.*

"Ahem," said Figby, "we are the legal and accounting firm of Figby, Migby, and Zarnoff, and we represent the estate of Rudy Frobisher."

"Ahem," said Migby, "we have examined his records and discovered one big mess."

"I'm not surprised," said Miss Hastings. "Mr. Frobisher is much too busy to keep things very neat."

"It's unfortunate he was so irresponsible," said Katrina Zarnoff, looking at Darius with big sad eyes that made him want to poke her in the nose.

"At least he's nice," said Darius.

"Was nice," said Figby.

"We are speaking in the past tense, unfortunately," said Migby. "Your father *was*, not is."

"I think he's still alive," said Darius.

"Not likely," said Katrina Zarnoff.

"But it's possible," insisted Darius.

"And pigs can fly," muttered Figby.

"Actually," said Darius, "my father once told me about a kind of pig he saw on a small island in the South Pacific. They live in trees and swing on vines, which is almost like flying."

Figby, Migby, and Zarnoff looked at Darius like he had three heads. They obviously thought he was as crazy as his father.

"Ahem." Figby cleared his throat and continued, "Unfortunately, although Mr. Frobisher sold insurance, he had none for himself. He took far too many risks for anyone to insure him."

"Ahem. And we have determined that the best thing to do is to sell the house and establish a trust for the young man," said Migby, ignoring both Darius and the housekeeper.

"We will distribute a modest amount of money to you, Miss Hastings, in recognition of your years of service," said Figby.

"And you, poor Darius," said Katrina Zarnoff, "what will we do with you?"

Suddenly the smell of something burning filled the room.

Katrina Zarnoff sniffed the air. "Is your house on fire?" she asked.

"Oh dear!" exclaimed Miss Hastings. "I forgot about the toast. I thought you might like some."

"I'll get it," said Darius. He got up and ran into the kitchen. Miss Hastings had been burning toast for years. While some people won't eat burnt toast, Darius had gotten used to the flavor and now quite liked it. He liked it even better because Miss Hastings made it for him.

He put the toast on a plate, cut it into neat triangles, and brought it into the living room. The three guests gave each other knowing looks, and then Katrina Zarnoff wrote something down on a notepad.

"No, thank you," they sniffed when Darius offered them some toast.

"It's really good," said Darius, taking a big bite. "I like it this way."

"As I was saying," said Katrina Zarnoff, "what will we do with you, little Darius?"

"You could leave me and Miss Hastings alone, and we could figure out what to do ourselves," Darius suggested.

The three visitors looked at the burnt toast on the table.

"Impossible," said Figby.

"Impracticable," said Migby.

"Out of the question!" proclaimed Katrina Zarnoff.

"Ahem," said Figby. "We have made arrangements for you to stay with the one relative you have left."

"Ahem," added Migby. "And you will be leaving tomorrow morning."

"You lucky boy," said Katrina Zarnoff, "You are going to live with your sweet Aunt Inga."

"Not that!" Darius nearly choked on his toast. "Anything but that! Anyone but Aunt Inga!"

"You're upset now," said the woman, "but time will heal your wounds."

"What about Miss Hastings?" said Darius, glancing over at his ancient caretaker. She had a very sad look on her face. "She needs me!"

"Don't be silly," said Figby. "She's a grown-up."

"She can take care of herself," said Migby.

"She burns the toast," said Darius.

"Then she shouldn't be raising you," said Katrina Zarnoff. "That's why we're sending you to your Aunt Inga. Tomorrow we will come for you. Pack a few things to take with you, but not too many. Your dear Aunt Inga doesn't have very much room in her house. She is making a sacrifice to take you in because she loves you." Katrina Zarnoff tried to pat Darius on the head. He leaned away from her to avoid her bony fingers.

"Aunt Inga doesn't even like me!" Darius protested.

But Figby, Migby, and Katrina Zarnoff were not listening. They snapped their briefcases shut and rose from their seats like a flock of scavengers, then flapped toward the door.

"We'll be back for you tomorrow," Figby squawked.

"Tomorrow morning," Migby added.

"Good-bye, Darius," said Katrina Zarnoff with a snooty smile. "And remember, this is for your own good." She then marched out of the house, Migby and Figby trailing in her wake.

"I told you," Darius called after them, "Aunt Inga doesn't even like me!" When he heard the door slam, he turned to Miss Hastings, who was now sitting on the couch.

There were tears running down her cheeks. "I am so sorry, Darius," she said.

"We can't let this happen!" said Darius.

But if there are two groups of people to whom unpleasant things happen despite their best efforts, it is children and old people. And as much as I would like it to be otherwise, Darius and Miss Hastings had more unpleasant things ahead.

Good-bye, Miss Hastings

After the lawyers left, Darius and Miss Hastings racked their brains trying to come up with a way out of their predicament.

"We could join the circus," Darius suggested.

"Yes, and I could be the lion tamer," said Miss Hastings.

Darius laughed. Miss Hastings smiled. Then they both fell silent again. Maybe pigs could fly, but Darius and Miss Hastings couldn't. Even if they could have, they had no place to land.

They sat at the kitchen table until the sun went down, but neither of them could think of a practical solution.

"Let's eat," said Miss Hastings. "Sometimes food helps."

Miss Hastings made a nice supper of macaroni and cheese and crispy brown toast, but neither of them felt like eating. "Darius, my dear," she said as she cleared away the dishes, "perhaps we should go to bed now and talk about all this tomorrow. Things always look better in the morning."

Darius suspected that Miss Hastings was putting on a brave face so he wouldn't feel so sad. He knew that Miss Hastings needed him, just as he needed her. Although they weren't related, Darius had always considered her part of his family. And now that his dad was gone, they only had each other.

You may be wondering where Darius's mother was in all of this. The sad fact is that Darius's mother had died years earlier in a horrible accident involving a can opener, an umbrella, and an English muffin. Darius had very little memory of her. Mr. Frobisher and Miss Hastings had raised him together.

Miss Hastings had been with Darius's family for many more years than Darius had been alive. In fact, she had been the family's housekeeper and babysitter when his father was born. No one knew how old she was. Even I don't, and I am telling the story.

More than being family, though, Miss Hastings was Darius's friend. When his father went on his stunning and ridiculously spectacular expeditions, Darius stayed home. Of course, he would have liked to travel with his father, but he didn't mind one bit being left with Miss Hastings. Darius's father was exciting, but Miss Hastings was like—well, she was like hot chocolate. She was endlessly kind and fun to be around, which is a high recommendation indeed for a housekeeper.

And she was a wonderful storyteller. Her stories were marvelous, even though they sometimes got muddled in the middle. Halfway through the story about Jack and the Beanstalk, Rapunzel might let her hair down from the giant's castle so Jack could climb in and have some of the bear's porridge. Darius fondly recalled many happy hours sitting forward on his chair and listening very closely to her miraculous tales. At the end of every story, Darius would always ask, "Is that true?"

"If it's not true, Darius," Miss Hastings would answer in a soft voice, "it should be."

Miss Hastings was also very good at making paper airplanes. Her room was on the third floor of the rambling old house, and she and Darius would fold huge pieces of paper into airplanes and launch them out of her window. As you know, they also enjoyed shooting water balloons off the roof.

And now they would both be leaving the big house. No more paper airplanes, no more balloons. Darius sighed and trudged up the stairs to his room.

Unable to sleep, Darius slipped into the hallway. The house was quiet. He tiptoed from room to room, counting the good memories about each one, as if each room were a book that held stories. At last, he came to his favorite—the Map Room. Several massive bookcases of rich dark wood were filled with atlases containing maps of every country, every ocean, every city, village, and hamlet ever known, as well as maps of stars, planets, and the moon. Three globes of different sizes stood on stands next to a heavy oak table. Maps covered the walls and the ceiling; someone had even painted a map of South America on the floor. A large grandfather clock in the corner ticked off each second and solemnly chimed every hour.

When Darius's father was getting ready for a trip, he would call Darius and Miss Hastings into the Map Room, pull an atlas from the shelf, and open it on the table. Then together they would locate his next destination. Darius grew to love maps as much as his father did. The maps were flat and made up only of lines and squiggles and words, but when Darius looked at them he saw forests and oceans and mountains, and even bustling city streets. He liked to imagine that he was flying over the land, looking down at the world below.

"If you can read a map," said his father, "you'll never be lost."

But that night, surrounded by maps and globes, Darius felt

very lost. He wondered how he was going to find his way without his father or Miss Hastings.

As if summoned by his thoughts, Miss Hastings came in the room. "There you are, Darius," she said.

Darius felt unspeakably sad. Miss Hastings walked over to a globe and gave it a spin. As it wobbled and squeaked, Darius closed his eyes and let his finger hover close to the spinning globe. This was a game that he used to play with his father and Miss Hastings, making up stories about where he would go when he was older. When the globe came to a stop, he opened his eyes to see where his finger was pointing.

"Vladivostok!" he said. "I'll go to Vladivostok!"

"And I'll go with you!" said Miss Hastings. She always said that.

They smiled at each other, but it wasn't the same. Darius's father wasn't there to make it seem like it really might happen. His father would have said something like this: *I have friends in Vladivostok! They have pet wolves! How would you like to play with a pet wolf? They don't bite!*

"Maybe you should pick out a book to take with you to Aunt Inga's," said Miss Hastings. "Your favorite map book?"

"I need a map for life," Darius muttered.

Unfortunately, none of the books on the shelves had one of those.

"You will be fine, Darius," Miss Hastings said.

Darius looked at her. "But what about you, Miss Hastings? Where will you go?"

"Oh," she said, "I will find a place. Don't you worry about me. I have some friends who I think will take me in."

But Darius was worried. What would she do? Friends were

fine, but as far as he knew, she had no family of her own; she'd spent her entire life taking care of the Frobishers.

"Miss Hastings, why didn't you get married? Why didn't you have your own kids, instead of just raising my dad and me?"

Miss Hastings slumped down in a chair by the globe. The clock ticked in the stillness.

Darius instantly wished he had kept his mouth shut. "I...I'm sorry," he stammered. "I just meant..."

"I almost did once," she said. A distant look came into her eyes, and she began to rub a small charm around her neck. It was a set of tiny silver wings. Even when he was quite young, Darius had noticed that Miss Hastings would reach for them when she seemed to be deep in thought.

"What happened?" Now Darius was too curious to keep his mouth shut.

"It didn't work out," she said sadly.

"Why didn't it work out?" Darius pressed her. "What happened? What was his name?"

"Oh, I don't want to talk about that," she said. "It was a long, long time ago, but it still makes me sad. I got mad at him because he did something I didn't like. I wouldn't talk to him. And then he wouldn't talk to me. And then he moved away."

"Did you ever see him again?" Darius asked.

"No," she said. "We went on with our lives, and, well, I was raising your father and taking care of the house, and both of us were proud. Too proud." She was still rubbing the wings.

Darius reached out and touched the charm with his finger. "Are these angel wings?" he asked.

"Oh no, they're just wings."

"Where'd you get them?"

"Well," said Miss Hastings, taking in a breath, "I got them from the person we were just talking about. When he gave them to me he said, 'Remember, you can fly.'"

"So you still like him."

"Oh no." Miss Hastings chuckled. "Nothing like that."

"Maybe you should look for him," said Darius.

"I'm afraid it's too late for that," said Miss Hastings. "Now I'm just an old woman who throws water balloons and burns toast."

"That's why I love you, Miss Hastings," said Darius. He usually didn't say things like this, but he was very afraid that he wasn't going to see her again, and he didn't want to lose anyone else without telling them how he felt.

"I love you, too, Darius," Miss Hastings said. She kept rubbing the silver wings.

The next morning Figby, Migby, and Zarnoff drove up bright and early in their shiny black sedan.

I'll bet I know what you are thinking. You are probably wishing they had never come.

You are probably wishing that they'd had four flat tires and their car was stuck in a ditch somewhere. Permanently.

Or that a pterodactyl had dropped down out of the sky, picked them up, and carried them far away, never to be seen again.

But that would be another story, not this one.

No, I'm afraid they showed up at the front door looking more crow-like than ever before. Miss Hastings was still dressed in her bathrobe and was wearing one sneaker. She looked horrible, and Darius was terribly worried about her.

"Can't I stay here?" said Darius, hoping the lawyers might change their minds.

"Of course not. Miss Hastings can't take care of you. She is known for burning toast," said Figby.

Migby opened up his briefcase and asked Miss Hastings to sign some papers.

"I don't want to sign them," she said. "I don't understand what they say."

"You wouldn't understand them anyway, even if we explained them," said Katrina Zarnoff. "Just sign. It's what's best for Darius."

Miss Hastings was sweet and loving and a wonderful story-teller, but she was not strong. So, she signed the papers.

"Run get your bags," said Katrina Zarnoff. "We don't want to be late."

Darius went upstairs to get his small suitcase. In it he had stuffed his most comfortable clothes and four books. Two were his favorite adventure books, which he had read many times. The third was the old book he had chosen the night before, the one containing small maps of every part of the world. The last was *Bullfinch's Mythology*, a book about monsters, gods, and heroes from some other time. His father had read it to him once long ago, although Darius had never read it himself. He didn't remember the stories as much as he remembered his father's voice.

Darius would have liked to pack more books, but he knew he couldn't take everything. He desperately hoped that if he only took one bag there would be room in the trunk of the car for one more thing: the bike his father had given him.

As Darius lugged the suitcase down the stairs, it bumped

against every step as if it were trying to stay where it thought it belonged.

Figby led everyone outside and put the suitcase in the trunk of the car. Darius hesitated a moment, then dashed into the garage to get his bicycle. When he wheeled it out, Figby, Migby, and Zarnoff all frowned.

"No bicycles," said Figby.

"I have to take my bicycle," said Darius. "My father gave it to me."

"No room," said Migby.

"But it's the only thing I own that I care about," Darius moaned.

"You poor dear," said Zarnoff. "You can get another one...sometime...maybe."

"Please!" begged Miss Hastings. "You can't take a bike away from a child who has no parents!"

Figby, Migby, and Zarnoff looked at Miss Hastings like she had just landed in an alien spaceship.

"It's just a bicycle!" they all said at the same time.

But a bicycle is not just a bicycle when your father gave it to you and then disappeared in a hot air balloon. It is a sad thing that these three grown-ups were too dull and blind to see that. I wish I could change them, but I can only tell this story the way it happened.

And what happened next was that Darius put his bike back in the garage and walked over to give Miss Hastings a hug. All his life, Miss Hastings had been bigger than he was, but as he wrapped his arms around her, he thought she seemed very small. She was crying. After they pulled away from each other, Miss Hastings reached back and undid the clasp of the chain that held the silver wings. She held it out to Darius. "I want you to have this," she said, blinking the tears from her eyes.

"No," said Darius, "I can't. It's yours."

"It's so you'll remember me."

"I'll always remember you!" said Darius.

Miss Hastings put the necklace in his hand and closed his fingers over it.

Darius slid the silver charm into his pocket, then kissed Miss Hastings on the cheek and gave her another tight hug.

"Ahem," said Figby.

"Ahem," said Migby.

"I'm sorry, but we're late," said Katrina Zarnoff, pulling Darius away. "It's not good for this poor boy to stay any longer."

"I'll write," called Miss Hastings.

Darius waved one last time before Katrina Zarnoff pushed him into the backseat of the shiny black car. As they drove away, Darius pressed his face against the car window and watched Miss Hastings grow smaller and smaller. When the car turned the corner, the housekeeper and the house disappeared entirely.

"What will happen to her?" he asked.

"She can take care of herself," said Katrina Zarnoff.

"You're wrong," said Darius. "She needs me. And I need her."

But no one answered, and the car drove on, leaving nearly everything Darius loved behind.

Ahead, unfortunately, was Aunt Inga.

3

Hello, Aunt Inga

Now it is time to say a word or two about Aunt Inga, even though it is an extremely unpleasant task.

Aunt Inga lived by herself in a town half a day away by car. Darius had been to her house a few times when he was very young. He didn't remember much about the visits except the disagreeable smell of boiled cabbage. Darius had never seen boiled cabbage in the house, which made him wonder if it weren't Aunt Inga who smelled that way.

The raw truth is that Aunt Inga was a miserable person. She made herself miserable and she made other people miserable, too. In Aunt Inga's mind, nothing was ever right, everything was always wrong, and things were only going to get worse. Her favorite saying—although she didn't know it—was, "I just knew that was going to happen." Aunt Inga always expected the worst, and she was never surprised when bad things occurred.

As great-aunts go, she wasn't terribly old, but her face was withered and worn. She wore her hair pulled up on top of her head, so her large ears stuck out like two cauliflowers.

So many things irritated her that it was hard to know what Aunt Inga *did* like. The only thing she didn't complain about was a special brand of little sandwich sugar cookies that came packed in a small white bag. She especially liked the chocolate filling in the middle. Every afternoon she sat in her overstuffed armchair and watched television while she ate cookies and drank tea. Her guests, on the rare occasions when she had any, had to fend for themselves.

Why was Aunt Inga so unpleasant?

I don't know.

Her niece, Darius's mother, hadn't been like that at all. It doesn't make much sense, but it's true. Even in the same family, people can be very different. Maybe, in your family, you are wonderful and perfect, while your brother or sister is the complete opposite. It's a strange world.

This all explains why Darius got more and more depressed as Figby, Migby, and Zarnoff's sleek black car carried him closer to his destination.

When they arrived at Aunt Inga's that afternoon, she was standing on the porch in a boldly flowered pink-and-green housecoat.

Katrina Zarnoff got out of the car and said in a cheery voice, "You must be Darius's Aunt Inga."

"I'm afraid so," Aunt Inga said with a frown.

Darius climbed out of the car. Aunt Inga shook her head as she looked at him. Her thin eyebrows, drawn on with a brown pencil, creased and uncreased. "Going to eat me out of house and home," she muttered.

"We will send you a check every month for expenses."

"You think this is just about money?" Aunt Inga groused. "Money's not enough to make up for all the trouble this will be."

"No, of course not," said Katrina Zarnoff.

"Of course not. I never planned on having any children. Didn't want them. What use do I have for children? Don't you think I have enough problems already? Don't you think I have enough on my plate?"

No one responded to her. There were no right answers. Figby, Migby, and Zarnoff handed over Darius and his suitcase as quickly as possible and made their getaway.

"Good luck, Darius," Katrina Zarnoff chirped as she backed the car out of the driveway.

"Good luck, Darius," Aunt Inga mimicked in a nasty tone. *"I'm the one who needs good luck, and I haven't had any yet. Not one ounce of it."* She looked Darius up and down disapprovingly. "Well, what am I going to do with you now?"

Darius had left home hours ago. It was now midafternoon and he hadn't had lunch. His stomach was grumbling and growling.

"Do you think I could have a little lunch?" he asked politely. "We didn't eat on the trip."

"I knew it! I just knew it!" Aunt Inga groaned, throwing her arms up in the air. "Hasn't been here five minutes and wants to eat me out of house and home. Well, you'll have to wait for dinner. I can't be preparing you food every half hour. I just won't do it."

Darius tried to explain. "I just wanted a little something—"

"I know what you wanted," Aunt Inga interrupted, shaking her bony finger in Darius's face. "You wanted to turn my whole life upside down, and you're going to do it one little snack at a time. Well, nosiree Bob. You'll just have to wait and eat at suppertime like a normal human being, not like some spoiled little child."

"I'm not spoiled," said Darius.

"Oh no? Not spoiled? Of course not! Father running around the planet, bringing you whatever you please. A servant to entertain you whenever you want. Not spoiled? No, spoiled rotten is what you really are! But that's all going to end here and now. I can't help that your parents are both gone. But I can help straighten some things out, and you're about to learn that life is not just about you. Nosiree Bob, I don't have time to wait on you hand and foot all day."

Darius stood there, thinking things couldn't get a whole lot worse.

And just at that moment, Aunt Inga looked up and smiled.

Darius turned to see what she was smiling at. A very large woman as big as a tank was trundling across the street. Riding in circles around her, slouched over a bicycle much too small for him, was a teenage boy. He wore a sour expression on his face.

"Hello, Gertrude," said Aunt Inga. She grabbed Darius by the arm and held him out in front of her. "Do you see what I mean?"

The woman looked at Darius and grimaced. "You're right. He's not much," she answered. "He's not anything at all like my Anthony." The boy on the bicycle came to a stop beside the woman. She stroked his arm.

"Anthony's home from military school for the summer," she purred. "Doesn't he look wonderful?"

He didn't look wonderful to Darius. He looked like a mean, pimply, skinny teenage boy hungry to do something horrible to anyone smaller than he was.

"Darius, these are our neighbors, Gertrude Gritbun and her son, Anthony. Say hello to them."

"Hello," said Darius.

"He doesn't look like much to me either, Mother," Anthony

21

sneered. Little bubbles of drool formed at the edges of his mouth as he spoke. "I've learned so much at military school. I'm sure I could teach him a thing or two this summer."

"Anthony, that's a wonderful idea," Aunt Inga said. She poked Darius in the ribs with her elbow. "Don't you have anything to say to Anthony's nice offer?"

Darius looked down at the ground. No words would come out of his mouth. Darius was an excellent judge of character—he knew he had been right about Aunt Inga, and he was not impressed with Anthony. What he wanted to say was, "You are both terribly, terribly mean." But he knew that would not help matters. Instead, he stood there without speaking, staring down at his shoes.

"I just knew it," Aunt Inga said. "Spoiled and rude, too. Oh, the burdens I have to carry, Gertrude."

"You poor dear," said Gertrude Gritbun. "It's good you're strong."

While his mother and Aunt Inga weren't looking, Anthony rode the front wheel of his bicycle over Darius's foot.

"Ow," said Darius. But the two women didn't seem to notice.

"Yes," said Aunt Inga, "and it's the strong that have to suffer. We'll see if we can't do something about him, won't we, Gertrude?"

"We certainly will," sniffed the stout woman. "Let's go, Anthony." As they turned to go, Anthony rode his bicycle over Darius's foot again and leaned toward him. Darius could smell Anthony's hot, bad breath as the bigger boy whispered in his ear.

"See you later, worm."

Anthony whipped his handlebars around and pedaled off. Mrs. Gritbun waddled along after him.

Aunt Inga turned to Darius and spit more angry words at him.

"I just knew it. There Anthony is, trying to make friends, whispering a little welcome to you, and you can't even respond. I'm embarrassed you're my relative. Pick up your things and come inside."

"I want to go home," said Darius.

"This *is* your home, little Mr. Snootypants," Aunt Inga snorted.

Darius followed his great-aunt into the house. What first struck Darius about the house was that the walls themselves seemed lonely—they were bare and pale, with no pictures of family, no art, no maps. The house was smaller than it looked from outside, and Darius couldn't imagine where he was going to sleep. Certainly, he hoped, not in the same room with Aunt Inga.

He shouldn't have worried.

Aunt Inga led him through the living room, which was completely taken up with a couch, an overstuffed chair, a small coffee table, and a large television set. The TV was on, filling the room with the sounds of a commercial about floor wax. A half-empty bag of the cookies Aunt Inga liked lay on the table. Darius followed her into the kitchen and down a few steps that led to the back door. He wondered if she was leading him outside. But then she turned and unlocked a side door that opened to a dark stairway.

"You'll have to sleep down there," Inga said. "I have no other room for you."

"In the basement?" Darius asked.

"I just knew it!" she said. "Here's a boy who doesn't have a home, and I offer him mine, but it's not good enough for him. Maybe you'd like me to give up my own bed? Is that what you want?"

"No," said Darius.

"Well, it doesn't make much difference what you want,

23

because you're lucky to have anything at all. This was not my idea. I didn't want to take you. 'There's no one else!' they said. And so here I am stuck with an ungrateful nine-year-old boy—"

"I'm eleven," said Darius.

"Don't correct me. I don't care if you're forty-six. There's a cot down there for you. At least it's cool. And if you're staying here, that's where you'll sleep. And I guess you will stay here, because no one else wants you. You can take your things down by yourself. I'm already behind with the million other things I had to do today. And don't ask for food until suppertime."

Aunt Inga put her hands on her hips and waited for Darius to move. He lifted his suitcase and lugged it down the basement stairs one step at a time. As he reached the bottom he heard Aunt Inga muttering to herself, "Thinks he's Mr. Snootypants. Like I don't have anything else to do but serve him hand and foot. I knew this was going to happen."

One dim light bulb hung over his head, casting long wavering shadows. In the corner beside a workbench was a small cot with a thin mattress and threadbare blanket. The pillow had no pillowcase. Darius put the suitcase next to the cot, sat down, and dropped his head into his hands.

"I have to get out of here," he said out loud. "I have to find Miss Hastings."

"I heard that," Aunt Inga called from the top of the stairs. Then Darius heard footsteps over his head. The noise of the television came through the floorboards.

Darius lay down on the cot. He reached in his pants pocket and pulled out the silver wings. Holding them close to his face, he ran his fingers over them, wondering if he would ever see Miss Hastings again.

Before he knew it, he had fallen asleep.

Darius Makes a Discovery

4

Things looked bleak for Darius. I wish they hadn't, and you may too.

You may be wishing that Darius would wake up back at home with Miss Hastings and find that moving in with his aunt was all a dream.

Or that Aunt Inga had just had a bad day, and today she would wake him with a kiss and a large breakfast of waffles, strawberries, and seven pounds of whipped cream.

Or that Darius, while sleeping, somehow acquired magic powers and turned Aunt Inga into a goldfish that lived on fish flakes, not cookies.

But none of those things happen. Not in this story.

Instead, Darius awoke the next morning in a musty basement on a cot with a thin mattress and threadbare blanket. His stomach was screaming for food. Still wearing his clothes from the day before, he tiptoed up the basement stairs.

On the top step he found a plate of food. Aunt Inga must have left it there for him the night before. On the plate was a small, dried-up pork patty, some overcooked green beans, and a stale piece of bread. Darius was starving, but he wasn't desperate enough to eat this. He opened the door and peered into the hallway. Seeing no sign of his aunt, he slipped into the kitchen.

The sun was streaming through the windows over the sink. Outside, he could hear the twitter of birds in the trees, the drone of a lawnmower, and the occasional *vroom* of a truck or car passing down the street.

Darius looked at the clock on the kitchen wall. It was almost eight-thirty. Was Aunt Inga already up and out of the house? He walked quietly through the living room, where he thought he heard a faint buzzing and hissing. Following the sound down another hallway, he came to a closed door. He pressed his ear against it and listened—the buzzing and hissing was definitely louder. Darius realized it was the moist and resonant sound of Aunt Inga snoring.

Darius didn't know that adults slept late. His father and Miss Hastings were always up before the sun every morning. Darius was usually an early riser, too, but he was rarely the first one up in his house.

He tiptoed back through the living room to the kitchen. Now his stomach was rumbling loud enough to wake even Aunt Inga. He pulled open the refrigerator. It was nearly empty—large bottles of soft drinks lined the door, and half a loaf of white bread, a stick of butter, and a jar of mayonnaise stood on the top shelf. The remains of a pound of bacon lay lonely in the meat drawer. The freezer was stuffed with frozen dinners. Looking through the cupboards, Darius found two cans of green beans and bag after bag of little cookies. He liked cookies, but not for breakfast. And anyway, he had a feeling that Aunt Inga kept track of exactly how many bags were in her cupboard.

Finally, Darius took two pieces of bread from the refrigerator and put them in the toaster. When they had browned to a dark and crunchy perfection—Miss Hastings would have been proud—he buttered them and carried them back downstairs.

Just as Darius reached the bottom of the steps, he stopped. A shaft of sunlight beamed down through the one basement window, and it shone into a gloomy corner like a golden spotlight. There, back in the cobwebs, Darius saw something that made his heart leap.

Stuffing the toast in his mouth, he crawled over old packing boxes and past a battered wardrobe until he came to the object highlighted by the sun. It was a very old bicycle, neglected and covered in cobwebs. The handlebars were rusty, and so were the wheel rims and spokes. The frame of the bike was a strange color of green that reminded Darius of the sea on a cloudy day. He tried to push it forward. Both tires were flat, and the bike seemed to weigh a ton.

Still, it was a bicycle.

Obviously no one had used it in years. Whose bike could it be? Never in a million years could Darius imagine Aunt Inga on a bicycle.

Darius thought of his own bicycle left behind. He clearly remembered that summer evening when he took his first ride on a two-wheeler.

He and his father had just finished dinner. The rays from the setting sun cast the trees and houses in a warm golden light. There was no traffic on their quiet street. Darius could hear only the hum of the crickets and cicadas as he climbed on the bike. How he loved its shiny red frame and silver fenders.

While Darius tried to balance himself, his father placed one hand on the back of the seat and the other on Darius's shoulder to steady him.

"Okay, flyboy," said his father, "you pedal and I'll hold on."

"What if I fall, Dad?" Darius asked.

"Don't worry," his father said. "Just give it your best try."

"But you told me you hurt your leg when you fell off a bike. That's why you limp!"

"That's true, son, I did have a bad fall," said his father. "When you are learning to do something new, you always run the risk of falling once or twice. That's how you grow."

That was a typical thing for Rudy Frobisher to say—he had tried many new things in his lifetime, and he was no longer afraid of falling.

"Anyway," his father went on, "I won't let you fall. You'll be fine."

Darius gripped the handlebars tightly. He felt his father's strong hands give the bike a push to get it going. Reassured by the unmistakable hiccupping sound of his father's limp and the ching ching ching of the coins bouncing in his pocket, Darius began to pedal. Then he felt his father's hand leave his shoulder.

"Don't let go, Dad!" Darius shouted.

"Keep pedaling!" his father yelled. "Go, flyboy, go!"

Darius pedaled harder, and the bike picked up speed, racing down the street. "Hold on to me, Dad!" he shrieked. "Hold on!"

And then he realized that he could no longer hear his father's hiccupping footsteps. He took a quick look back over his shoulder. His father was standing far behind him with his hands on his hips and a huge smile on his face.

"Pedal!" his father urged. "Pedal, and watch where you're going. Always watch where you're going!"

A shudder of excitement ran through Darius as he realized that he was riding on his own. He felt balanced, in control, yet somehow completely free from the world around him. He had often dreamed of soaring above the clouds, but this was no dream. He felt both terrified and exhilarated.

"Yippeee!" Darius was nearing the end of the block with no idea how to turn around and afraid to try. Somehow he managed a wobbly, twisting turn and headed back toward his father, who was still urging him on.

"Come home, flyboy! Come on back! All on your own!"

The loud honk of a horn on the street startled Darius out of his daydream. He wasn't riding a bike with his father—he was standing in Aunt Inga's dirty, musty, stinky basement. But he was looking at a real bicycle, lying unused, in need of a rider.

Darius made a path through the boxes and pulled the bike across the basement, shoving it around the old wardrobe. After several tries, he finally managed to push the bike up the basement stairs and out the back door.

In the daylight, Darius could see that the bike was in bad shape. Not only were the wheels flat and the rims rusted, but the fenders were dented so badly that they scraped the wheels when they rolled. The chain was rusted, and the seat was badly tattered and worn.

But Darius also saw that the situation was not hopeless. With a little hard work, he could fix it up and use it. He could already picture himself flying along the street, racing farther and farther from Aunt Inga's house.

And so, the makings of a plan came to Darius. I'll fix this bike, he thought. I'll ride away from Aunt Inga and never come back. I'll find Miss Hastings, and we'll take care of each other.

He knew it wouldn't be easy. Miss Hastings was very far away. As a matter of fact, Darius wasn't sure just where she would be living since the lawyers had kicked her out of the house. She'd said she had a place to stay, some friends somewhere in the town where Darius had grown up. But where?

Really, it was a ridiculous idea, fixing up an old bike and riding hundreds of miles to find a very old woman who burns toast. Where would he sleep on the way? What would he eat? The chances of pulling it off were a million to one.

But it was a dream, and when things are this bad a person needs some kind of dream.

He thought about his father. Finding him was a dream, too, but Darius didn't have the faintest idea of how to make it come true. Even if he knew where to look, how would he get there? Sneak on board a freighter? Find his own hot air balloon? Build a giant kite? No. He decided the first step would be to find Miss Hastings. If anyone could help him find Rudy Frobisher, it was his beloved housekeeper.

For now, fixing the bicycle and finding Miss Hastings would have to be enough.

Darius decided to carry the bike back down the stairs and keep it in the basement. He thought about asking Aunt Inga if he could fix it. But if he asked, then Aunt Inga would know he wanted the bike, and she didn't seem likely to give him anything he wanted. If she said no, Darius thought he would die. He decided it was better not to ask. The bike would be his secret.

I know what you are thinking.

WHAT IF HE GETS CAUGHT?

Good question. Carrying a heavy old bike up and down the basement stairs makes a lot of noise. You're probably wondering why Aunt Inga hadn't heard all the racket. Even Darius wondered why she hadn't burst into the kitchen, demanding to know what had been going on.

The reason is that Aunt Inga was still sound asleep. She always got her best sleep from six to ten every morning. During the early hours of the night, she would lie awake and think about all the things that were wrong and all the things that might go wrong next week or next year. Finally, just before dawn she would doze off, exhausted. And when she slept, she slept like a log. Right until ten o'clock in the morning, which is late indeed, unless you are a teenager.

The rest of the day, Aunt Inga walked around in her pink-and-green housecoat, unless she had to go to the store, which she did every Wednesday.

Aunt Inga's house was small. The living room, kitchen, and her bedroom occupied the entire first floor. Two tiny rooms upstairs were filled almost to the ceiling with things she had bought and saved but never used. She rarely went upstairs anymore and never went into the basement. And she hardly ever went outdoors, except for shopping or to visit in the yard with her neighbor Mrs. Gritbun.

Aunt Inga didn't have to go out because she worked at home on her own schedule. She sat in the big chair in front of the television and made phone calls, trying to get people to buy subscriptions to magazines nobody wanted. She persuaded a lot of people to buy them because she was so pushy and annoying. As you know, it can be hard to say no to someone who is pushy and annoying. Some people would buy even the stupidest magazines from Aunt Inga just to get off the phone with her.

Her sales pitch went something like this:

"Yes, I'm calling for the American Magazine Company. Believe me, I don't like making these calls any more than you like getting them. You can imagine how difficult it is to call people I don't know, but how else am I going to get by? My time is as valuable as yours, so let's get on with it. You may not like it, but I'm just going to keep calling, so you might as well quit stalling and order some magazines now.

"Only one? That's it? All right, but there's no reason to make my job so difficult. I'm just trying to help everybody here, but nobody ever appreciates it. I'll just put you down for a couple of extra subscriptions.

"Sure, go ahead. Eat your dinner while I have to stay here and work. Fine. Good-bye."

She sold a lot of magazines.

Aunt Inga was so good at making people feel like idiots, she only had to make phone calls in her big chair in front of the television for three hours a day. She liked to call in the late afternoon and early evening, when she knew people were sitting down to eat dinner with their families.

It worked like a charm. Aunt Inga had dozens of golden plaques from the magazine companies thanking her for selling magazines that nobody wanted.

When Aunt Inga wasn't on the phone selling magazines, she sat in her big chair and watched television and ate cookies and took little naps. The television was on from ten o'clock in the morning, when she woke up, till eleven-thirty at night, when she went to bed.

The only thing that could tear Aunt Inga away from her chair in front of the TV was the mail. Every afternoon at exactly a quarter past two, Aunt Inga stood at the front door waiting for the mailman. If he was late, she let him know what an inconvenience it was for her. And of course, the mail always disappointed her.

"Nothing. Nothing but people wanting me to buy things I don't need. Do they think I don't have anything better to do with my time than open their dumb envelopes?"

You may be thinking it's odd that she hated being bothered by people wanting her to buy things she didn't need, when that is exactly what she did for a living. Me too. But some people are just like that.

So, Aunt Inga didn't hear Darius when he took the bike up and down the basement stairs. It's a good thing, because I'm sure, just as Darius was, that she wouldn't have let him touch the bike, even though no one was using it.

Aunt Inga didn't know the first thing about bikes. She couldn't ride a bike if she had to. To be sure, she had learned how to ride a bike when she was a little girl. But even though everyone says that once you ride a bike, you never forget how, I am afraid that she had.

You are probably wishing that Aunt Inga would just stop being mean and say, "Darius, my little bunnykins, anything you find in that musty old basement is yours."

But you know Aunt Inga well enough by now to know that she's not going to say anything of the sort.

33

5
A Strange Occurrence

Darius survived the next few days, but that was about all he did. It seemed that Aunt Inga was doing her best to forget that he was there.

And then, on the fourth day at Aunt Inga's, a very strange thing happened.

It was quite early and Darius was sitting in the dim basement with his head in his hands, staring at the bike again. It was in worse shape than he thought.

"I can't do this," he said to himself, "it's impossible! I'll have to live with Aunt Inga forever!"

He climbed up the stairs and went out the door into the backyard. Absentmindedly, he stuck his hands in his pockets. His fingers touched the chain that Miss Hastings had given him. He pulled it out and held it up. The silver wings dangled in front of his face.

As he gazed at the charm, he heard a clanking and a whirring. He instantly recognized the sound of a pedal arm hitting the chain guard on every turn, and the clicking of a derailleur. It was someone riding a bicycle. He looked around. Where was the noise coming from? Darius ran around the house and peered up and down the street. No one was there. Now the sound was above him. He looked up into the sky.

"Holy moly!" he gasped.

There, forty feet above the houses, was an old man riding a bicycle unlike any Darius had ever seen. Extra parts had been attached to every available surface. Someone had welded forks to the fenders, and the forks held smaller wheels that spun upside down in the air. Strange wing-like contraptions extended from the handlebars and wheel hubs.

Darius stared at the man flying the bicycle. A mane of white hair stuck out from underneath a black skateboard helmet. The man's long, sky-blue coat fluttered in the wind behind him like a cape. The rider was humming loudly as the bike disappeared over the trees.

Then it was over. What Darius had seen lasted no more than nine or ten seconds. He ran down the street, hoping for another look, just to make sure that what he had seen was real. But the sky was now empty; there was nothing but a few wispy clouds high overhead and a sparrow winging its way skyward.

Because of his father's adventures and stories, Darius had come to believe that almost anything was possible. But he had never imagined a flying bicycle.

Maybe I saw it because it was really there, he thought, *or maybe I saw it because I wanted to see it.*

Darius couldn't be sure. "Maybe I'm just going crazy," he said out loud.

Maybe he was.

Later that day, his head still reeling with the vision of a flying bicycle and the disappointment over the broken bike in the corner, Darius lay on his cot, staring at the basement ceiling. When he heard the floorboards creak over his head, he guessed that it was a quarter past two, and that his aunt was making her way to the front door to get the mail. He heard Aunt Inga's voice. Although he couldn't hear what she said, he could tell by the tone of her voice that she was scolding the mailman again. The door slammed, and the footsteps returned to the living room.

It suddenly occurred to Darius that Miss Hastings hadn't written him like she'd promised. Maybe she hadn't had time at first after her move. Maybe she was walking to the post office to mail him a letter right now. Or maybe she had already written to him!

Darius crept upstairs and peeped into the living room. Aunt Inga was back in her big chair, opening her mail, watching television, and nibbling on cookies. Darius knew this was not a good time to talk to his aunt. But there was never a good time to talk to her.

"Aunt Inga," he said as politely as he could, "has Miss Hastings written to me?"

"What?" Aunt Inga said.

"Has Miss Hastings written me any letters?" he asked, moving closer to her and trying to make himself heard over the raucous TV applause.

"Fine," Aunt Inga grumbled, looking up. "Now he thinks I'm in charge of mail delivery. How would I know if she has written? Have you gotten anything?"

"No, but I just thought..." He paused for a moment, then said, "Maybe I should write to her."

"Do you know her address?" Aunt Inga asked.

"Well, no. But maybe we could find it out."

"And how would we do that? I don't know where she went. It would be a wild goose chase. You need to get on with your life and stop wishing things were what they used to be. You're lucky you're here. You have a roof over your head and plenty to eat. There's a woman here on television who had to feed her children dog food. Have I ever fed you dog food?"

"No..." said Darius, thinking about the plate of warmed-over pork patties and clammy green beans she'd left for him every evening since his arrival.

"Exactly. Now please don't disturb me." She turned back to watching the program, fumbling in a bag for another cookie. Darius watched for a while—it was a talk show with people arguing about the horrible things they had done to each other.

"That's right," Aunt Inga said to the talk show host. "You tell him. Running off like that without saying good-bye and taking the vacuum cleaner, too. I'd stick him in the slammer and throw away the key!"

The television shows Aunt Inga watched only reinforced her belief that people were, by and large, rotten creatures. She looked back at Darius.

"You see how the world is? What's the point of trying to do any good? What do I get for all my pains? I take you in, and here you are worried about getting letters from some old woman. Always thinking of yourself, Mr. Snootypants."

Darius decided that if he ever got to be in charge, grown-ups would have to take a test to prove that they liked kids before they would be allowed to take care of them. Only nice people would raise children.

Aunt Inga would have failed the test and had her license denied.

Darius went into the kitchen to escape the lecture. But Aunt

Inga only raised her voice. "Fine!" she shouted. "Go in there and eat my food, too. I knew that would happen. Why don't you go outside and do something? You'll never make anything of yourself sitting around here."

For once, Darius thought Aunt Inga was making sense. Glad for an excuse to get away from her, he slipped out the back door. Darius heard some whooping and shouting. He rounded the corner of the house just in time to see Anthony riding by furiously on his bicycle. In the middle of the street, directly in front of Aunt Inga's, was a ramp made of a sheet of plywood, one end propped up on some milk crates.

Anthony pedaled up the ramp at top speed. "Yee-haaaaah!" he yelled. The wheels spun wildly as the bike left the ramp and flew through the air. The bicycle landed, *thump, thump,* and Anthony careened down the street, then circled back for another try. Even though he had the very strong feeling that Anthony was showing off just to taunt him, Darius couldn't help but watch. He longed for a bike of his own—one that he could ride, not that rusty wreck he'd found in the basement.

"Too bad you don't have a bike," Anthony chortled as he circled around again. "If you did, you could fly like me. But maybe it's just as well. You'd never be as good as I am."

Darius watched the older boy pop wheelies and weave up and down the street. Darius was desperate to ride. Finally, he got up enough courage to speak.

"Anthony, can I ride your bike?"

"No," the boy replied, "I'm putting it away now and going inside. If you want, you can watch TV with me. But you can't talk when the show's on."

"What show are you going to watch?" Darius asked.

"I don't know," Anthony answered, "Whatever's on."

Darius didn't want to watch television. But he was bored out of his mind, and he didn't want to go back to Aunt Inga's house.

Anthony's house was bigger than Aunt Inga's, although most of the time the family didn't need the extra space. Mr. Gritbun worked on top-secret computer projects and only came home once every three months for a shower and breakfast. During the school year, Anthony was at military school.

You may be wondering why the Gritbuns sent their son away to school.

Anthony Gritbun was, to put it mildly, a handful. At home, he rarely did what he was told and often did exactly what he was told *not* to do. I suppose that is one reason his parents sent him away. The other reason was this: Anthony's father had gone to Crapper Military Academy, and he wanted his son to go there, too.

"Look at me," Mr. Gritbun had said one day during breakfast, just before he disappeared for another three months. "I turned out all right. A few years at Crapper will do wonders for our boy."

Anthony had spent the past nine months at Crapper, but so far it was hard to tell just what wonders the school had worked on him.

Anthony led Darius into his bedroom and turned on the television. It was a stupid movie about a policeman who lost his job and fell in love with a woman who was going to rob a bank because she needed money for her child who had to have an operation. There was much more kissing than there needed to be, and Darius was bored. Every time there was a commercial, Anthony stopped staring at the tube and jumped on Darius. He held him down and hit him on top of the head with his sharp knuckles.

"Ouch!" said Darius. "Stop it! That hurts."

Anthony laughed. "They do it harder than that at school. Do you want to see what else they do?"

"NO!!" Darius yelled. Just then, the commercial ended. Suddenly, Anthony climbed off Darius, sat back down, and stared at the set.

At the next commercial, Anthony said, "Where was I? Oh, that's right. The Laundry Job! Do you know what a Laundry Job is?"

"No," said Darius, "and I don't want to—"

Before he could finish, Anthony leapt onto Darius's back, grabbed the back of Darius's underpants and pulled on them until they reached almost over Darius's head. Anthony guffawed. "That's a Laundry Job, you worm. I learned it at school." With Anthony sitting on top of him and his underwear stretched to its limit, Darius could only hold his breath and wait. When the commercial ended, Anthony climbed off of Darius and stared at the television again. Darius stuffed his stretched underwear back in his pants, then tiptoed out the door. Anthony's eyes never left the TV screen.

Darius walked through the living room and out the front door, which he closed quietly behind him. He decided that from then on he would avoid Anthony whenever possible.

Avoiding Anthony *and* Aunt Inga meant that Darius spent most of his time in the basement or the backyard.

Early every morning he worked on the old bike with a few rusty hand tools he had scavenged from Aunt Inga's garage. On nice days, he dragged the bike out into the backyard, where he could work in the fresh air. About the time he thought his aunt would be waking up, he'd put away the bike and the tools and wait in the basement until she called him for breakfast.

He'd then spend the next few hours on his cot, reading and rereading the books he'd brought with him. He had nearly memorized the adventure books. He stared at the maps in the atlas, imagining he was somewhere else. The book his father had read to him, *Bullfinch's Mythology,* was difficult; he tried to imagine his father's voice reading the words, and that made it easier.

Darius was trapped. And he was bored. Bored as could be.

Although you may not like to admit it, I'm sure you've been bored in the summer. There are too many hours in the day, and there is no way to get where you want to go to do something interesting. If you could drive and had an endless supply of money, you'd go to the water park on Monday, to the zoo on Tuesday, and to the beach on Wednesday, and you'd never get bored. But when you can't drive and you don't have much money, you stay at home and get bored. And you drive the people around you crazy. Even if they love you.

But since the only person around was Aunt Inga, Darius

thought *he* might go crazy. His aunt didn't want Darius in the house, but she didn't want him out of the house either. Really, she just didn't want him anywhere. If he stayed in the basement, she would say, "Where have you been? You think you can just hide out down there without so much as a word as to what you're doing? Here I am, so worried about what you're up to that I can't get anything else done."

Then, when he came upstairs and sat quietly while his aunt watched TV or made her phone calls, she would say, "Fine, Mr. Snootypants, you just sit there and stare at me. You don't do anything worthwhile the whole day long. I don't know why I put up with you. I'm here slaving away and you don't lift a finger to help out."

Darius had read about slaves, and Aunt Inga didn't appear to be slaving away at anything.

After a while, Darius realized that he was going to disappoint her no matter what he did.

So one day, just when he was about to go crazy with boredom, he slipped through the kitchen and called from the back door, "I'm going out!" Then he left before her tirade began.

Darius waited at the corner of the house until he could hear Anthony at the other end of the street. When the coast was clear, he hurried in the opposite direction, past the neighboring houses and a gas station on the corner. Crossing a busy street, he wandered around for half an hour, but didn't find a single park or even a shady spot where he could get out of the hot sun.

Finally, Darius turned and headed to Aunt Inga's. "I might as well give up," he said to himself. "I could search forever in this neighborhood and nothing good would come of it.

However, on the way back, something good did happen.

Darius found the library.

More Books and Bikes

D arius hadn't noticed the library before—maybe he just took a wrong turn, which became a right turn. The building stood back from the street, and a sidewalk, shaded by trees, led to its front doors.

As soon as Darius walked into the library, he felt himself relax—it was quiet and cool, and people spoke softly in tones very different from the ones he heard from Aunt Inga.

"May I help you?" a woman behind the desk asked.

"No thank you," Darius said. "I'm just looking."

He found the children's section and started to look through the shelves of books. But after several minutes, an idea formed in his mind. He went up to the desk, where he saw a nameplate with "Ms. Gloria Bickerstaff" printed on it.

"Excuse me, Ms. Bickerstaff," he said.

"Yes?" she answered brightly.

"Do you have any maps?"

"Of course we have maps. We have books and books of maps—they're called atlases."

"Yes ma'am, I know that," he said. "My name is Darius, and before my father disappeared, we had a map room in the house where I used to live."

"My goodness," Ms. Bickerstaff said, catching her breath. "I'm sorry to hear about your father. But how wonderful to have a map room in your home. We have a map room here, too!"

"You do? Honest?" Darius couldn't believe his ears.

"Honest," she said, pointing past Darius's shoulder. "Back to the left, through those doors."

Darius walked across the main room and peered through the doors. A globe stood in the corner of the small room. Copies of ancient maps covered one wall. He was delighted to see that the shelves held large books the size of card tables, and several atlases were spread across the reading tables, opened to maps much more detailed and colorful than the ones in his own book. And the smell! How he loved the glorious smell of books! He had known that smell his whole life. This was the closest he had felt to home since leaving Miss Hastings.

Darius lost track of time in the map room. Finally, he found a map that showed both Aunt Inga's and his old town. He used the map scale to measure the miles between the two.

"Two hundred forty-six miles. Let's see, if I rode a bike twenty-five miles a day...," Darius muttered. He picked up a short yellow pencil and scribbled the numbers on a scrap piece of paper. "...it would take me ten days to get to Miss Hastings."

If he could find Miss Hastings!

He wondered where she lived now.

Darius left the map room and approached Ms. Bickerstaff's desk again. She was reading a book. "Excuse me, ma'am," he said softly.

The librarian looked up and smiled. "Yes, Darius," she answered. Darius's heart warmed at the sound of her kind voice saying his name.

"Do you think you could help me find somebody? I'm looking for her address."

"Well, we could search for it on the computer. What's her name?"

"Miss Hastings. I know her first name is Grace."

"What town?"

Darius told her the name of the town where he used to live.

"Let's see what we can find," the librarian said. Darius followed Ms. Bickerstaff to the computer and stood by her side as her fingers flew over the keys. For all the music and stories and maps and adventures in Darius's life, he hadn't had much experience with computers. He was glad to be with someone who had. His spirits rose as Ms. Bickerstaff continued to search. But finally, she shook her head.

"I'm not finding anything, Darius," Ms. Bickerstaff said. "Maybe she doesn't have a new phone or address yet."

"Maybe not," Darius said, his heart sinking. "She might be living with someone else. I'll just have to keep looking."

Before he left, Ms. Bickerstaff gave Darius a library card, then helped him pick out an atlas and two books about travel adventures to take home. He wanted to take some of the large atlases, but Ms. Bickerstaff said he'd have to read them in the library. "Those are reference books. They stay here."

"I'd like to stay here, too," said Darius.

Ms. Bickerstaff laughed. She thought he was kidding. She didn't know he really meant it.

"Let me know if I can help with anything else, Darius," she added.

"Sure," he answered. "Thanks." As he headed out of the library, he could feel Ms. Bickerstaff watching him. Without even thinking, he reached in his pocket and pulled out the silver wings Miss Hastings had given him. "I'm going to find you!" he whispered.

It seemed silly and ridiculous to think that he could fix the old bike in the basement, escape Aunt Inga, ride for ten days, find Miss Hastings, and run away with her.

"It sure would help if the bike flew," Darius said to himself, looking up at the sky. It seemed almost impossible that he would ever get there.

But when you're desperate, almost impossible is not bad odds.

Darius should have stayed in the library. As he lugged the books up the back stairs into the house, he heard Aunt Inga's voice over the blare of the television.

"Where have you been?" she called.

Darius stuck his head into the living room and found her holding her hand over the receiver of the phone.

"I went to the library," he said, holding out the books. "I got these."

"Without my permission?" she asked.

"Well, um...yes," said Darius.

"Fine. Just fine." She uncovered the mouthpiece and spoke to someone. "I'm sorry. I'll have to call you back.... Yes. Of course I will. If you know what's good for you, you'll take three subscriptions.... Of course I'll bother to call you. I have to. Do you think I like this?"

She hung up.

"Now look what you've made me do. I've lost at least three

subscriptions and probably won't get them back, all because you bothered me. What's all this about the library?"

"I got some books to look at."

"Well, you'll just take them right back. I don't want all of your books and things cluttering up my house."

"I'll be careful. I'll keep them downstairs."

"Sure you will. I know how this goes. You'll forget all about them, and you know who'll end up paying the months and months of fines? Do you? I'll tell you who. Me. I knew this was going to happen—one burden after another falling on me. Every single book will go back tomorrow, or you won't be going to the library at all. One more thing for me to keep an eye on. I just knew it. Now let me get back to work."

Tears filled Darius's eyes. "I'm keeping the books!" he said, almost shouting. "You don't have to worry. I'll take them back on time."

Aunt Inga began to sputter. "Oh, well, look at Mr. Snootypants now. Been here one week and thinks he's ruling the roost. Thinks he can do whatever he wants at my expense."

"I just want to look at these library books!"

"You will take those library books back tomorrow! This is my house and I won't have any books in here cluttering up the place, making it look like a *pig sty!*"

The walls rattled with Aunt Inga's shrill voice.

"All right, all right," Darius said, turning to escape to the basement. "Sorry."

"SORRY. NOW HE'S SAYING HE'S SORRY! NOW THAT EVERYTHING IS IN AN UPROAR, HE'S SAYING HE'S SORRY. A LOT OF GOOD THAT DOES. COMES IN, RUINS MY BUSINESS, EATS ME OUT OF HOUSE AND HOME, AND MAKES

THE HOUSE A DISASTER AREA, BRINGING THINGS IN WITHOUT MY PERMISSION. AND WHAT DO I GET FOR THIS? WHAT'S MY REWARD? NOTHING. ABSOLUTELY NOTHING!"

Aunt Inga went on yelling, lost in her own world. She didn't even notice that Darius had left the room.

In the basement, he lay down on his cot and looked at the library books while Aunt Inga continued her tirade. It was hard to concentrate, but he had no trouble locating the map that showed the road leading from Aunt Inga's to his old town. He stared at the map until it was burned into his brain cells.

"I've got to get out of here soon," said Darius to himself. "I'll have to work even harder to fix that bike."

He rolled over and sat up on the edge of the cot. The silver wings in his pocket jabbed his leg, and Miss Hastings's words echoed in his head. "We all have wings."

He wished he had wings to fly right now, but all he had was a bike that he couldn't ride.

Not yet, at least.

The next day, he took the books back to the library. Ms. Bickerstaff recognized him the moment he came in.

"Back so soon, Darius?" she asked.

"Yes," he said. "I'm done with the books."

He held them out to her, but she didn't take them. "You can have them for two weeks," she said. "Why are you bringing them back?"

Darius didn't want to explain. How could he? "There's not enough room where I live for me to keep them there," he said.

That sounded absurd, and he knew it. But Ms. Bickerstaff didn't tell him that. Instead she looked at him thoughtfully and smiled.

"I have an idea," she said. She took the books and rose from her chair. "We have an extra empty shelf here behind the desk. We'll make this your shelf, since no one's using it. The books you take out from the library, you can keep here."

Darius caught his breath. "Really?"

"Really," Ms. Bickerstaff said, smiling again.

"Thanks," said Darius. "I have to go."

"They'll be here waiting for you," she said.

Darius turned and walked out of the library. He smiled as he thought about the librarian's kindness. Even though she knew something was wrong, she had helped him without asking for an explanation. That is about as kind as anyone can get, he thought.

Darius got up early every morning, made three pieces of toast, and put peanut butter on them. He sat on the back steps, eating his breakfast.

Everything seemed peaceful then, and he liked watching the sun come up. During that quiet time alone, Darius tinkered on the old bicycle. He would bring the bike up the stairs and work on it in the backyard for a couple of hours, then take it back down to the basement before Aunt Inga woke up.

One day he found some aluminum foil in a kitchen drawer and rubbed it on the handlebars to take off the rust. Another day he filled a bucket with soapy water and washed the frame. He found an oilcan in the basement and oiled the chain.

The bike began to look better.

But Aunt Inga began to get suspicious.

"What are you doing every morning before I get up?" she asked him.

"Nothing," answered Darius. Aunt Inga was sitting in her big chair, stuffing cookies in her mouth and watching a game show while she talked to him. Aunt Inga should have weighed four hundred pounds from all those cookies, but she was still skinny as a rail.

"Don't give me that," Aunt Inga snorted. "You must be doing something. I don't want you to go outside before I'm up. I can't trust you. And why was the kitchen sponge wet this morning?"

"I was wiping up the sink with it," said Darius.

"Well, just don't do anything without telling me," she said, cookie crumbs spraying from her mouth. "Now don't bother me; this is a very important show."

Darius went down into the basement. He found an old blanket and carefully covered the bike. If it was a secret, it had better stay hidden. He couldn't afford to let anyone see it—not if he was going to use it to find Miss Hastings.

It had been almost two weeks since Darius had found the old bicycle in the basement. As he worked on the bike, he started to think of it as his. That can happen with things—when you care for them, they become a part of you. Darius often daydreamed about the places he would go with the bike and the things he would do.

One night, in his dreams, Darius climbed on the newly repaired bicycle and pedaled madly. The frame had been painted the impossible turquoise of the ocean in the tropics. The bike went faster and faster, and then, suddenly, Darius was in the air, pedaling over the houses and roads, looking down at the earth beneath him. It looked like an enormous map! The names of cities and rivers and countries were printed on the land he flew over. The word "Newfoundland" spread out below him across forests and plains. He remembered that Newfoundland was the last place his father had been seen before he'd disappeared over the ocean. Darius looked out across the horizon. Off in the distance he saw a balloon of blue and orange and red and yellow stripes. His father was in it—waving to him!

"There he is!" someone behind him said. The bike had become a tandem bike, and Miss Hastings was on the seat behind him, pedaling.

"Let's go get him!" she shouted.

"Dad, here I am!" Darius yelled. "I'm coming, Dad. Wait for me."

And then he woke up on his thin mattress in the basement.

Finally, the bike was all ready, except for the tires. They were still as flat as could be. Darius pushed the bike up the stairs and out the back door, and walked it down the driveway. He planned to take the bike to the gas station on the corner, fill the tires, and then ride back to the house. He would be back in plenty of time before Aunt Inga woke up and turned on the television.

But when Darius reached the gas station, he discovered that the air pump was broken. He remembered another station several blocks away, so he pushed the bike there. But he ran into another problem—to make the air pump work, you had to put in two quarters. He didn't even have a dime.

Now he began to worry about the time. Darius certainly didn't want Aunt Inga finding out about the bike when he had just gotten it ready to use.

"Excuse me," Darius asked the man inside. "I don't have any money and I really need to fill up my tires. Is there any way of making the pump work without putting money in?"

The man looked at Darius like he was crazy. "What do you think this is, kid, a place for free handouts?"

"How can you charge fifty cents for air?" asked Darius. "Air should be free!"

"Get outta here, kid," said the gas station attendant. "Go get some money from your mom."

Darius didn't bother to explain that that was impossible. He went back outside, sat down with his bike on the curb, and thought. He remembered one other service station, but it was all the way over by the library. Darius looked at his watch. If he hurried, he might be able to fill the tires and ride back before Aunt Inga got up.

I know what you are thinking. It would have been more sensible to go back to the house and wait until the next morning. But if you had been working patiently on a bicycle for days and days, what would you have done?

I bet you couldn't help yourself, and neither could Darius.

He set off, moving as quickly as he could. It wasn't easy pushing a bike with two flat tires.

And it was further than he thought. By the time he got to the third gas station, it was 9:45. Darius had fifteen minutes to get the tires filled and get the bike safely hidden away.

Little beads of sweat began to run down his back as he thought about what would happen if Aunt Inga found him gone. He dragged the bike over to the air pump and put the nozzle on the tire valves one at a time.

"*Hssssssss,*" screamed the air hose.

"*Clang, clang, clang,*" rang the air pump's bell.

As the tires swelled with air, the bike seemed to rise up off the pavement. Darius hung the air hose back on the rack and looked at the bike. It was ready to ride. He hopped on and took off down the street. The gears clicked and whirred as he pushed the pedals faster and faster. Darius felt like a million bucks.

"YEEE-HAAAAH!" he screamed as he turned a corner. "This is a piece of cake! I'll be back in no time!"

And that is when the most horrible thing happened.

7
Enter Daedalus

uddenly Darius's feet spun on the pedals and he heard a grinding, clanking sound, as if something were scraping on the pavement. He looked down. The bicycle chain had broken and was caught in the teeth of the sprocket. Sparks flew up as the chain dragged and bounced along the street. The bike veered to the side and the front tire hit the curb. Darius flew head over heels above the handlebars and landed on someone's lawn. The bicycle careened into the gutter, teetered for a moment on one wheel, then slowly tipped over into the street.

Darius waited until his head stopped spinning, then got up and brushed himself off. He'd scraped his arms and elbows, but he wasn't really hurt—it was the bicycle that worried him. His heart was pounding as he ran over to the bike. He pulled it onto the sidewalk and looked at the damage. The rim of the front wheel was a little bent, but it still turned. Some spokes were twisted. Worst of all was the chain. He huddled over the bike, holding the greasy chain in both hands, trying to figure out how to make them go together.

"Oh no," he moaned, "Aunt Inga will eat me alive."

Tears welled up in his eyes.

"She's going to kill me," he wailed. "She's going to—"

"Broken chain?" boomed a deep voice just behind him.

Darius looked up from the bike. His heart almost stopped.

An old man holding a black skateboard helmet in one hand was staring at him. He was dressed in baggy clothes—wrinkled khaki pants and an oversized white shirt. A long, sky-blue coat hung down to his shoes. Even the man's hair seemed baggy: although the top of his head was bald, long shanks of white hair streamed down over his ears. His eyes were crystal blue, and his nose was long and a little red around the edges. The odd-looking man was sitting on an old three-speed bicycle. A large basket attached to the handlebars held vegetables and a loaf of bread, as if he had just been grocery shopping.

Darius knew exactly who this was. It was the man who had flown over his house on the bicycle! "I've seen you before," he said. "You were riding a flying bike."

"Impossible," said the man, his eyebrows working up and down as he spoke. "Inconceivable. It was probably your imagination."

"I don't think so," said Darius, shaking his head.

"Your bicycle is broken." The man seemed eager to change the topic of conversation.

"Yes, sir," said Darius, remembering the desperate spot he was in. He tried to push the chain together. "My dumb chain broke and there's no way to fix it. I'll never get back in time now."

"Well," the man said with a strange grin on his face, "let's see what I have here."

He reached into a pouch strapped around his waist and fumbled through it. "Ah, here we are," he said, pulling out a little tool that glinted in the sunlight. "Chain wrench. Works wonders," he cackled.

He bent down and took the chain from Darius's hands. He

slipped the contraption on the chain, wound it tight, popped the chain back together, and tightened it. He pulled the chain on the sprocket and stood the bike up.

"All fixed now. You can ride it, but you'd better get the rim fixed soon."

Darius looked up in wonder. "Who are you?"

"Daedalus."

"Deh-dah-lus?"

"That's correct. And your name?"

"Darius. What kind of name is Daedalus?"

"Ancient Greek. I'm not really ancient, though. Old, but not ancient. And I'm not Greek, either. You'd better get going if you don't want to get eaten by this Aunt Inga you were moaning about. She sounds like Hera on a bad day."

"Hera, I think I've heard that name," said Darius. He seemed to remember his father reading to him about her.

"Hera was queen of the gods! She was married to Zeus. He was the big cheese of all the gods, but he wasn't very dependable. Hera was always getting mad at him. Just like Aunt Inga—whoever she is—will be, if you don't get going."

Darius looked at his watch. It was 9:54. His heart jumped.

"Thanks, Daedalus." He threw the words over his shoulder as he hopped on his bike. Darius took off, the pedals clanking and the chain whirring.

"Fix the rim," Daedalus called after him. "And get a helmet. One bump on the noggin and you're kaput."

Darius pumped the pedals madly, turning to the right at the first intersection, then to the left at the next corner. Time was running out. The bike was moving, but the front wheel wobbled and would not turn freely. As he swerved onto his own street, with one hundred yards to go, the bell in the church at the end of the street began to ring the hour. It was ten o'clock.

Aunt Inga was getting up!

The television was about to go on!

He was about to be eaten alive!

Darius tore up the driveway and flung himself off the bike. Standing outside the back door, he tried to calm down and catch his breath. He opened the door quietly and listened. There was no sound. As carefully as he could, he pulled the bike through the doorway and onto the basement steps. Halfway down, he heard his aunt's footsteps as she walked over the floorboards. He scooted down the last few steps and paused, listening again. All was quiet. Then, from the top of the stairs, he heard Aunt Inga's voice.

"Darius! Darius! Are you down there?" she called.

"Yes, Aunt Inga."

"Well, what are you doing?"

Darius tried to quiet his breathing. "Nothing," he called up the stairs.

"Then why is the back door open? Where have you been? I'd better come down there and see what you're up to."

Darius heard Aunt Inga's foot hit the top step.

"No, wait!" Darius screamed. If Aunt Inga came down now, his goose was cooked. Darius frantically kicked off his shoes and pulled off his shorts. He ran to the bottom of the stairs and stood there in his underwear, looking up at the gaunt figure of Aunt Inga silhouetted against the light from the open door.

"Don't come down just yet, Aunt Inga," he begged. "I'm in my underwear."

Aunt Inga looked away. "Oh, what a disgusting creature. Put

your clothes on this instant. Have you no decency at all? Look what I have to put up with!" Aunt Inga turned away and pulled herself back into the hallway. "You've got me so upset I'm going to be late getting my breakfast, and I'll miss the beginning of *Moneymania*."

"Yes, Aunt Inga, I'll be right up."

Darius stood motionless as he listened to Aunt Inga's footsteps over his head, going into the living room. He was sure that if his aunt stopped to listen, she would hear his heart beating, leaping, catapulting out of his chest. Then he heard the television go on. Darius let out a long, loud sigh. He was safe in the basement.

And so was his bicycle.

Remote Control

8

That very afternoon, Darius made a very useful discovery. Aunt Inga had gone shopping, and he was alone when he heard a knock.

When Darius opened the front door, Anthony walked right into the house without being asked.

"Hi, you little worm," the boy sneered.

"Hello, Anthony."

"My mom sent me over here to be nice to you," Anthony said, pushing his way past Darius.

Darius hurried after him into the kitchen, where his rude neighbor was already opening and shutting cupboards.

"Where are those cookies your aunt is always eating? Ah, here they are." Anthony took down a bag, tore it open, and pulled out a handful. He stuffed three cookies in his mouth.

"Wait, Anthony," Darius said. "You can't do that. She'll know there's some missing."

"And whose problem is that?"

"She'll kill me."

"Exactly. Like I said, not my problem." He took out another handful, then handed Darius the near-empty bag. "If you're going to die, you might as well have some."

Darius put the bag on the counter and went back into the living room. Anthony followed, his mouth and hands filled with cookies, and hovered inches away from Darius—much too close for his liking. "What were you doing?" Anthony asked. "Probably something stupid."

"I was reading a book."

"Something stupid, just like I thought," said Anthony. "At Crapper Academy we don't have time to read. There are too many important things to do."

Darius was mystified. He liked reading, and he assumed that's what all kids did at school. "You don't read books?" he asked.

"Oh, some, sure.... One or two."

"Then what do you do?" asked Darius.

"Important things. Like drilling and marching. I'm especially good at drilling—a lot better than you'll ever be. We polish buttons on our uniforms and get ready for inspections. And we have meetings about discipline and order. Discipline and order are very important."

"Why is discipline important?"

This question upset Anthony. He started circling around Darius, leaning over him and yelling, "Why is it important? What kind of idiot are you? Don't you know anything? If there's no discipline, everything falls apart. Soon the enemy would come and take over!"

"Who is the enemy?" asked Darius, trying to move out of range of Anthony's terrible breath.

"Who's the enemy? You're even stupider than I thought," said Anthony, backing Darius down into Aunt Inga's big chair. "The enemy could be anybody, anytime. You know, if you went to Crapper Academy, you'd probably be under disciplinary arrest all the time."

"Disciplinary arrest? What's that?"

Anthony shrieked with laughter. "What's that? WHAT'S THAT? It's when you can't do anything right, and they have to punish you. Half the school is under arrest all the time! You'd be under arrest the minute you got there, that's for sure."

Darius shuddered. "What happens to you when you're under arrest? How can they arrest so many kids?"

"A special squad of students is chosen to guard them, and *we're* in charge of punishment." Anthony leaned very close and smiled. "I'm going to be captain of the guards next year. I'll get to decide what the punishments are."

Darius was thinking that Crapper sounded like the most unpleasant school in the universe, when all of a sudden Anthony pounced on top of him and started twisting his arm. "Let's wrestle," he said. "I'm sure I can wrestle better than you can."

"Ouch! Stop it!" yelled Darius. Anthony was twisting his arm so hard that Darius was afraid he would twist it off. Darius squirmed and struggled, trying to get away.

"Stop it, Anthony! Stop it!" he yelled, but Anthony only laughed louder. Darius looked around in desperation, trying to think of a way to stop this torture. The only thing within his reach was the television remote control. With his one free hand, he grabbed it and pushed the ON button.

"Anthony," he screamed, "let's watch some television."

The second the television came on, Anthony let go of Darius and sank to the floor, staring at the screen.

Darius looked at Anthony. The boy's eyes were glazed over. Darius turned off the television. Anthony instantly came back to life and leered at Darius.

"I'll twist your arm off, just like I do to kids at school," he cackled, reaching toward Darius.

Darius hit the ON button again. Anthony slumped back to the ground and stared at the screen.

TV off. Anthony came to life. TV on. Anthony stared.

It was magic! This is a handy little trick, Darius thought. He left the television on and headed to the library for his daily visit, leaving Anthony in the room, staring in silence as the television chattered on.

Over the next several days, early every morning, Darius tried to fix the bent rim. He took the wheel off the bike and clamped it in a vise bolted to the worktable in the basement. But when he tried to bend the rim straight with a pair of pliers, he only made it worse. If you've ever tried to get something back into shape after it's bent, you know that it can be as hard as getting toothpaste back in the tube after you have squirted out too much. The wheel grew more and more twisted, and the spokes began to look like day-old, dried-up spaghetti.

"Oh, boogers!" said Darius, growing more and more frustrated. Every morning at ten o'clock, he had to stop working and wait until the next day, when the wheel problem seemed even more impossible to solve. One morning he sat on the basement steps looking at the mangled wheel in his hands, completely empty of hope. "I'll never get this fixed," he moaned. "I need help. I need to find that guy, Daedalus."

But he had no idea where to look.

The next morning, Darius woke extra early and walked back to the spot where he had met the strange man. It was just an ordinary corner in the middle of an ordinary neighborhood. There was nothing around that had anything to do with a man who fixed bicycles and flew through the air. Darius sat on the curb watching the traffic. He waited as long as he could, hoping Daedalus might come by. But not one single flying bicycle appeared.

"Daedalus," he said to himself, "I know his name is Daedalus."

He could think of only one person in the town who might be able to help him.

"I'm going to the library, Aunt Inga," he said that afternoon.

"Fine," grumbled his aunt, not looking up from her television show. "Go off and do as you please. It's all you ever do anyway. But don't be dragging any books back into this house and cluttering up my home with your mess."

The library is a nice place for anyone, but it seemed particularly welcome to Darius that day. The children's section was almost empty, and Ms. Bickerstaff was behind her desk.

"Hello, Darius," she said. "How can I help you today?"

"I need to find someone named Daedalus," Darius said. "Can you help me?"

"Do you mean the man who flew?"

"Yes! Yes!" Darius said. "Do you know him?" He couldn't believe it. "Have you seen him fly?"

Ms. Bickerstaff laughed. "No, I've never seen him fly. And if he really did, it was thousands of years ago."

"What do you mean?" Darius asked. Now he was really confused. "I just met him the other day."

"Well, I don't know about that," said the librarian. "The Daedalus I know is in a Greek myth. Do you know the story?"

"No," said Darius. He was disappointed that Ms. Bickerstaff

didn't know the Daedalus who flew on a bike. Still, he *was* interested in the story. "Can you tell it to me?"

"Yes, I can," said Ms. Bickerstaff. And she did.

Feathers and Wax

9

Darius sat down on a chair by the desk. Ms. Bickerstaff put her elbows on the desk and leaned toward him. She lowered her voice and whispered the story like it was a secret.

"Daedalus was a master craftsman and inventor. He lived on the island of Crete in the Mediterranean Sea. King Minos ordered him to build a labyrinth, an elaborate maze, to imprison the minotaur."

"What's a minotaur?" asked Darius.

"A creature with the head of a bull and the body of a man. And not nice at all. It ate children."

"Just children?"

"Adults, too. Anything."

"Yikes," said Darius.

"Exactly!" said Ms. Bickerstaff. "Daedalus built a labyrinth so winding and complicated that the minotaur couldn't get out. And they say that Daedalus invented sails for boats, too."

"Pretty smart," said Darius. A builder and an inventor. The story made him think of the Daedalus who had fixed his bicycle chain.

"Right again, Darius," said Ms. Bickerstaff. "And he had a son named Icarus, whom he loved very much."

Darius smiled.

Ms. Bickerstaff went on with the story. "But King Minos learned that Daedalus had once betrayed him, so he had him locked away. And then Daedalus did the most amazing thing." She stopped, looking at Darius with dancing eyes.

"What? What did he do?"

"He built wings to fly! He made them of bird feathers and wax and string. One pair for himself and one for his son."

"His son was in prison with him?"

"Yes! Daedalus planned for them to escape together. When he put the wings on his son he said, Icarus, when we fly with these wings, don't fly too close to the sun. The wax will melt and you'll fall."

Now Darius knew it was just a story. You would have to fly millions of miles to get close to the sun. But that didn't bother him at all. When you're listening to a good story, you can ignore little things like how far away the sun really is. "What did Icarus do?" asked Darius.

"He didn't listen. He was too excited about flying. Or perhaps he thought he knew everything. Who knows?" said Ms. Bickerstaff, holding her hands, palms up, in the air.

"I bet he was a teenager!" said Darius. "I know someone just like that!"

"Yes," laughed Ms. Bickerstaff, "he probably was a teenager. He probably rolled his eyes and said, 'Sure, sure, sure, whatever you say. Just let me fly.'"

"Then what?"

"Daedalus and Icarus took off. The wings worked! Soon they

were over the prison walls and soaring out over the sea. I think it must have been beautiful. Can't you just imagine it? The sun was shining, and the sky was blue, and so was the sea. And the wind was rushing through the feathers of the wings. It would be wonderful to fly like that."

Darius nodded. It *would* be wonderful.

"They flew on and on. Daedalus loved flying. But Icarus was completely entranced. 'Look at me!' he yelled. And he flew higher and higher."

"Oh no!" Darius exclaimed.

"Oh yes!" said Ms. Bickerstaff. "Icarus was so fascinated with flying that he forgot about the ground. He forgot he was just a boy. He forgot his wings were made of feathers and wax. He forgot what his father said.

"'Icarus, come back!' Daedalus called to him. 'Don't fly any higher!' But Icarus still didn't listen. Maybe he was too far away already. Maybe he was in the spell of the sun and the wind and the sea. But he flew higher and higher. The wax melted. The feathers fell out. And then he fell into the sea."

Darius's eyes filled with tears. At first Ms. Bickerstaff didn't notice. She went on with the story.

"Daedalus tried to find him. But his son was lost in the ocean. Daedalus never saw him again."

Darius tried not to cry, but he couldn't help it.

"Oh dear," said Ms. Bickerstaff. "What have I done? What's wrong?" She reached out and touched Darius's arm.

"It's all right," said Darius, wiping his eyes with his sleeve. "It's okay. It's just a story, I know."

Ms. Bickerstaff handed Darius a tissue. "No, Darius," she said, softly but seriously, "you're wrong. Nothing is ever 'just a story.'

If a story speaks to you, then it can be a way to understand how and why things happen. I know that, because my whole life is about stories, real and imaginary. And they're all important."

They were both quiet for a moment.

Perhaps you think silence means nothing is happening. But often, silence means more than words. Words are wonderful, but, as you may have discovered yourself, sometimes they aren't enough.

Finally, Darius spoke. "It's a good story," he said.

"Yes," said Ms. Bickerstaff, patting his arm.

"It reminds me of my dad."

"I see." Ms. Bickerstaff knew that more words were of no use right then.

Darius sat up straight in his chair. "I still need to find a real person named Daedalus," he said. "He lives around here somewhere. He fixed my bicycle."

"Oh! Why didn't you tell me before I went on and on about that myth? Let's see. We can look in the phone book," said Ms. Bickerstaff. "Does he have a last name?"

"I don't know. I just know his name is Daedalus."

"If we don't know his last name, we'll have to look a little harder. It will be our own little labyrinth, with Daedalus waiting at the end. Come on over here to the computer and let's see what we can find."

It was like finding the way out of a maze. For the next ten minutes, Ms. Bickerstaff's fingers danced over the keyboard. When her search came to a dead end, she tried another route. Finally, a name popped up on the screen. The first name was Daedalus. The last name was Panforth. He lived on a street called Magnolia Terrace.

"Do you know where that is?" asked Ms. Bickerstaff.

"No," said Darius, "but I can find it on a map."

And he did.

As Darius was leaving the library, Ms. Bickerstaff held out a book. "Can you take just one book home?" she asked.

"I can try," Darius said, taking the large book in his hands. The cover showed a man flying above the earth in a chariot being pulled by four white horses, and the title was *D'Aulaire's Book of Greek Myths*. Darius opened the book. It was old and worn—the pages were soft and frayed on the edges—it had been read many times. He turned to the first page. "In olden times," it began, "when men still worshipped ugly idols, there lived in the land of Greece a folk of shepherds and herdsmen who cherished light and beauty."

That sounded good to him.

"Thanks," said Darius. "Thanks for everything."

"You're very welcome, Darius," said Ms. Bickerstaff. Darius noticed the smile on her face, but he didn't see the tears in her eyes.

You're probably wishing that Ms. Bickerstaff would stop Darius and ask him out to lunch, and he could tell her his whole story, and she would know just what to do.

Or that Ms. Bickerstaff would tell Darius that he could sleep in the library in a featherbed surrounded by thousands of books.

Or that Ms. Bickerstaff was one of those rare librarians who was actually paid what she deserved for all of her hard work and that she would adopt Darius and he would come live in her huge mansion, also filled with thousands of books.

But none of those things happen in this story.

Darius did have a map now, though. And a wonderful book.

And an address for someone named Daedalus Panforth.

After a fifteen-minute walk, Darius turned onto Magnolia Terrace. The first thing he noticed was a hand-painted sign on a telephone pole.

DEAD END—BIKES ONLY

As he quickened his pace, he saw a girl pedaling toward him on a bike with training wheels. A man, most likely her father, ran along beside her.

"Excuse me," said Darius. "I'm looking for someone named Daedalus."

"End of the street," said the man as he ran by, "you can't miss it."

"Yippee!" said the girl. Darius watched the two of them until they disappeared around the corner.

When Darius turned back, he stopped in his tracks. His eyes bulged. His heart beat faster.

Down at the end of the short street sat a small house.

While the house itself was not spectacular, everything around it was.

The yard was overflowing with old bicycles of every description. They were lined up next to each other, stacked vertically, piled on top of one another, arranged so that there were little paths between the piles. An ancient picket fence with peeling white paint surrounded the yard, as if it were trying to keep the bikes from falling out of the yard onto the street. A few bike wheels hung over the fence, looking like they were trying to escape. The mailbox swung from the front forks of a bicycle frame that was stuck vertically into the ground.

Darius approached the house slowly, step by step, taking it all in. In one corner of the yard, under a cedar tree, he saw an enormous pile of handlebars. Fenders of every size, shape, and color lined the sidewalk. The porch was completely filled with wheels and tires, blocking the doorway. In the small side yard, a sculpture caught Darius's eye. Welded-together gears, sprockets, kickstands, and countless other bicycle parts towered twenty feet into the air.

In front of the sculpture was a neat row of bicycles. A sign hung on one of them.

> ### GOOD AS NEW. ALL BIKES $10.
> ### TRADE-INS ACCEPTED!

Darius thought this house was the most beautiful,
    wonderful,
        marvelous,
            and magnificent thing
               he had ever seen.

His heart raced, and a pure, simple laugh bubbled up from deep inside him.

"Hello there," a voice called out from somewhere above him. Darius looked up. Along the peak of the roof he saw another row of bikes lined up next to a tall antenna. Standing on top of the chimney, adjusting a bike on top of the antenna pole, was Daedalus, his white hair sticking out in all directions. He turned the bike he was holding this way and that, until he seemed to have it where he wanted. "There...," said Daedalus. "No, there. There...there...there!"

Darius stared.

Daedalus took his hands away from the bike, watching to see if it would stay. The bike teetered back and forth, then stopped, balanced perfectly on the metal rod.

"Perfect," Daedalus chortled. "This should help with the reception."

He looked down at Darius. "Meet me in the back," he called. He winked and disappeared on the other side of the roof.

Darius skirted the pile of handlebars and picked his way through the maze of bicycle remains. Like the front, the backyard was chock-full of bicycles, bicycle parts, and bicycle sculptures of every size and description. The old man was climbing down a trellis festooned with a jungle of vines. The large leaves sprawled out, hiding the porch like so many green elephant ears.

Daedalus leapt from the trellis and looked Darius up and down. The old man turned his head to one side and then the other, squinting his eyes as if he were looking to see if any parts had been put on in the wrong place. A quick grin broke out on his face.

"You found me," he said. "I thought you would."

Darius had been speechless ever since he had seen the house. But now he found his voice.

"I've been trying to find you! My rim is bent and I can't fix it!"

"Oho! Bent rim. That's right. It's the worst. I bet you tried to fix it and botched the job completely. I bet the spokes look like Medusa's hair! Nothing but a head full of snakes, you know! How'd you like to comb it?"

"A head full of snakes?" asked Darius.

"Right! That was after Venus got through with her. Venus, the goddess of beauty, was jealous of her, so she turned Medusa into an ugly monster. How ugly, you ask? She was so ugly that one look at her would turn you to stone."

"That's ugly," said Darius, nodding.

"Of course it is," said Daedalus. "The Greeks didn't mess around when it came to extremes." He stopped suddenly and pointed to the book under Darius's arm. "Greek myths! Excellent. That nice little volume is a good start, but..." He leaned forward and put his face close to Darius's and whispered mysteriously, "There is more. Much, much more! More horrible. More wonderful. I can tell you. I know." His eyebrows wiggled up and down as if they had lives of their own.

Daedalus straightened himself and paused a moment as if lost in thought, then he looked back at Darius, eyes bright and twinkling. "Now, listen, my young warrior—do your parents know where you are?"

"No," said Darius. "I don't have any parents. All I have now is Aunt Inga."

"Hmm, I remember. Like Hera—Zeus's wife."

"She doesn't have a husband. And she's kind of strict."

Daedalus scrunched up his face. "Well, all right. For the time being, you may come in, although I, too, am quite strict, at least about who works with me. Children shouldn't wander around without their parents' permission."

"I told you, I don't have any parents."

"Right. Right. Sorry to hear that. But for today—let's see. Twenty-six by one and a half, that's my guess. Come with me." He turned and walked up the steps, across the back porch, and into the house.

Darius took a deep breath and followed the strange and wonderful man inside.

10
Inside Daedalus's House

Inside the back door, Darius looked around. To his left he could see a kitchen, very simple and sparse, with dishes stacked in the sink. On the right was a small study. The shelves lining the walls were filled with books. Hundreds of other volumes stood piled on the floor and overflowed out into the small hallway.

Directly in front of him Darius saw Daedalus standing by a narrow doorway. The old man flipped on a light switch and started down a flight of stairs into the basement. Darius followed him, marveling at all the drawings and photographs taped and thumbtacked along the staircase walls. Every picture, whether it was a snapshot or a drawing made by children's hands, showed boys and girls smiling proudly beside their bicycles. He recognized Daedalus in many of the pictures.

Darius stepped down into the basement and looked around in surprise. It was the exact opposite of what he had seen on the outside. The basement was an immaculate and perfectly organized bicycle workshop. The magical space held every kind of bike part imaginable, placed in the most orderly fashion. Front forks had been hung with care from a rack on one wall, along with seats and sprockets and frames. Deflated inner tubes of different sizes had been neatly draped over a series of nails in the ceiling. Along another wall, clipped to a pegboard, was the most wonderful array of horns, lights, and bells Darius had ever seen. Above a long workbench against the far wall was another enormous pegboard covered with tools of every size and description. A bike stood on the workbench, half put together. Darius felt his body shake with excitement. He was sure he was dreaming.

"Wow," he said to himself, "this is bike heaven!"

"The discardings of a careless world, my good man," Daedalus said in a grand voice, "left for rag and bone pickers like me to save from the horrors of some gigantic landfill. Wasteful, wasteful! But then, it gives me something to do. I don't make much money. But I need little. The less I have, the less I have to worry about." Daedalus moved to the far corner of the workbench and turned on a radio. A man's voice boomed out, hitting an exceptionally high note. "There!" shouted Daedalus. "My adjustments to the antenna were successful! Listen—it's Puccini!"

"I've heard of him," said Darius. "My dad played opera for me all the time."

"Did he?" Daedalus asked enthusiastically. "What an excellent fellow!"

"Yes," said Darius, and for a moment, he could see his father in his imagination and hear the *ching ching ching* of the coins in his father's pocket. Something about being in this basement made his father seem close.

Daedalus turned off the radio. "Let's see." He reached up to a long rack of rims and sorted through them.

"Twenty-six by one and a half, twenty-six by one and a half," he mumbled to himself. Then he pulled off four or five rims and took down the one behind them.

"Twenty-six by one and a half," said Daedalus, handing it to Darius. "It's a bit worn, but perfectly round."

"Thanks," Darius murmured. "But I'm afraid I don't have any money."

"Oh, fine," laughed Daedalus, "another customer with no money!" He didn't seem to be at all bothered that Darius couldn't pay. "You hold on to that rim, my good man, while I finish a little job I was working on. In the meantime, feel free to look around."

Darius hardly knew where to look first. In this wonderful workshop all the bike parts seemed to be almost alive—each wheel and hub and frame carrying a promise of something that might be. He turned slowly, trying to take everything in. His eyes fell upon a picture hanging over the workbench. It was obviously old—the paper was yellowed and curled up at the corners. Darius stood on tiptoe and stared. It was a colored pencil drawing of a boy on a red bike. The bike was suspended in the air, supported by large balloons attached to each fender. Birds were flying around the boy on the bike, and the boy was waving his hand, wearing a very large smile.

"Who's that?" asked Darius. "Is it real?"

"What's real and what's true?" asked Daedalus. "They say that when Orpheus played on his harp, the trees walked nearer so they might hear him. Do you believe that?"

"I don't think so," he answered honestly.

"Then you miss the point entirely. It's not whether the trees could walk—it's how beautifully Orpheus played." Daedalus paused and looked up at the picture. "That's a boy's dream," he said. "That's what that is."

"What boy?"

"The boy in the picture, of course. Now, listen, you have your rim. Can you put it on yourself? I expect you can. And it's getting close to ten o'clock. Aren't you afraid of your Aunt Inga eating you alive?"

The mention of Aunt Inga brought Darius back to earth, away from the boy on the bike. "Omigosh, you're right. I have to go."

Darius headed for the steps, where he stopped again. There underneath the basement stairs, he saw the bike—the bizarre piece of machinery that Darius had seen Daedalus riding through the air over the housetops. He turned back to Daedalus.

"It was *you*, wasn't it? There's the bike you were riding! You know how to fly on a bike."

"Impossible," said Daedalus. "Inconceivable."

"But your bike was flying! That's a miracle! How do you do it?"

"I don't," answered Daedalus. "You saw nothing of the sort. Must be loony."

"But—" Darius began.

"No, not now. Some other time. You're about to be eaten—you'd better run."

"Okay, but can I come back?"

Daedalus looked intently at Darius, as if he were sizing him up.

"Please," begged Darius, "I could help you. I could pay you by working on bikes. You could teach me, and we could fix bikes together. And maybe I could work on my bike more. It's really still a big mess." Darius felt his cheeks grow hot. Had he said too much?

But Daedalus smiled. "Why not? Bring that old clunker of yours and we'll fix it up like new."

"I'll be your assistant," said Darius.

"Splendid!" said Daedalus. "My assistant. But you must come only in the morning. I work on bikes in the early morning. In the afternoon I read and think."

"What do you think about?"

Daedalus raised his eyebrows. "The universe," he answered.

"The whole universe?"

"As much of it as my brain will hold," Daedalus said. "There are dimensions most people have never dreamed of. I try to see them."

"Dimensions?"

"Dimensions. Aspects. Elements. Parts. I think if I could only see a couple more of them, then I could solve the problem of—" Daedalus stopped and looked at Darius. "Oh, enough of that. At any rate, while I'm trying to think about it, I can't be disturbed."

"Okay," said Darius. "It's better if I come early in the morning anyway, before Aunt Inga is up. That way she doesn't ask so many questions."

"Now, off with you, my young hero. Venture forth on the wine-dark sea! And next time, before you come, let your aunt know where you're going."

"Do I have to? I'm afraid she won't let me."

"You must tell her, if you want to come back."

"Yes, sir," said Darius. "Good-bye, Daedalus." He ran up the stairs, through the kitchen, and out into the yard filled with hundreds of bikes. Darius darted around the piles of bicycle parts, dashed outside the fence, and tore down the street, holding the rim in both hands.

He ran as though there were balloons tied to each arm, and wheels where his feet should have been.

He was that happy.

Meeting Daedalus was the best thing that had happened to Darius for a long, long time. Every morning Darius would sneak out of his house at six o'clock, stop at the bakery just as it opened, and pick up two cinnamon buns still warm from the oven, paying with the pocket money Daedalus had given him. Every morning Daedalus would be waiting for him at his kitchen table with a big pitcher of freshly squeezed orange juice. As they ate their breakfast, the old man told stories about the ancient Greeks. Darius loved listening to them.

"Were you named after the Daedalus in the book?" Darius asked.

"Hmmm. Could be," answered Daedalus, his eyes twinkling.

"How do you know all these stories?" asked Darius. "Were you there?"

Daedalus laughed out loud. "No, no, no, no....but I have lived with them for so long they are part of me. I learned these stories as a boy, and I still love them as a man."

Daedalus told Darius about the hero Perseus, flying over the ocean on winged shoes. He told about Phaëthon, the son of the god Apollo, driving the chariot holding the sun across the sky. He told about Hermes, zooming here and there, delivering messages for his father, Zeus, king of all the gods.

After the stories were told and the breakfast table was cleared, they would both go down into the basement to work.

Daedalus encouraged Darius to rebuild his bike from scratch.

"Can't we just fix the parts that really need fixing?" Darius asked. "I really want to ride my bike. I have big plans."

"All the more reason to rebuild it. Fix a flat and ride today. Rebuild a bike, and ride a lifetime."

Daedalus was laughing as he spoke, but Darius knew the old man was right. Darius didn't really mind taking the bike apart and putting it back together. Although he was desperate to escape from Aunt Inga's clutches, he loved his time with Daedalus. And Darius knew that if he was really going to ride all the way back to find Miss Hastings, the bike would have to be sturdy and strong.

Together they took the bike completely apart—the wheels, the handlebar, the chain, the sprocket, the ball bearings, the spokes—everything. Darius looked at all the parts spread across the floor in small, neat piles.

"I'll never get it back together," wailed Darius.

"Don't be a ninny," said Daedalus. "Of course you will. And once you learn to put this one together, you can take apart and reassemble just about any bike in my shop."

And soon Darius was able to help Daedalus with simple jobs on the bicycles that children had left at the shop for repair. Darius was happy for a way to repay Daedalus for the parts he needed and for all he was learning.

As he worked, Darius often looked at the strange flying bike under the stairs, wondering why Daedalus wouldn't answer his questions about it. And then one morning, Darius discovered another mystery. He was repairing a bike and needed a set of handlebars. None of the sets hanging on the walls seemed to fit. Daedalus was busy working on a wheel at his workbench, whistling to himself.

Thinking that he might find the right size handlebars, Darius began searching among the old bikes stored in the part of the basement behind the stairs. He went past the strange flying bicycle, into a dark corner where more old bike parts were stacked. Up against a wall near the furnace, he spotted a bike with a promising set of handlebars. Bicycle parts clattered and clanged as he pushed his way through.

"What are you doing back there?" Daedalus called.

"Looking for handlebars," Darius answered.

"There's nothing back there," said Daedalus.

"Yes, there is," said Darius. "I see an old bike up against the wall."

"Leave that one alone!" Daedalus snapped.

But it was too late. Darius had already started to pull it out into the dim light. The bike was red, faded by time and rust. There were several odd-looking attachments on the fenders. The front wheel was horribly bent and twisted, and the entire bike was very dusty, but otherwise it was in good shape.

"Hey," he said, "this looks like the red bicycle in the picture. It's just my size." Darius was trembling with excitement. "It wasn't a dream! It's real!"

Daedalus was standing a few feet away, looking at Darius.

"It would be perfect for me! Why don't we fix it? Then I can ride it."

"No," sighed Daedalus.

"Why not?"

"Because you might fall and hurt yourself," Daedalus said.

"But that's not a good reason! My dad told me that when you do something new you always risk falling a few times."

"It's a better reason than you know," said Daedalus. "Now leave the bicycle there and don't ask again."

"Why won't you fix it?"

"I will not talk about it, and you have no right to ask. Please come out of there now, and don't ask again." Daedalus spoke sternly, in a voice Darius had never heard him use before. Darius could tell that was the end of the conversation. But he knew it was not the end of the story.

In the days that followed, he tried to bring up the flying bicycle in the drawing again and again, but Daedalus always refused to talk about it. Darius looked at the picture over Daedalus's workbench of the boy on the bicycle. He wished it were he—flying to find Miss Hastings. And then off to Newfoundland, to look for his father.

But Darius had to content himself with working on the old bike from Aunt Inga's basement and helping Daedalus fix the bikes children brought in almost every morning.

"How do all those kids find you?" Darius asked. "How do they know you'll help them? Do you put up signs?"

"Of course not," said Daedalus. "Too much trouble. Do I look that ambitious? I've found that word of mouth counts for everything—if someone needs me they'll find me. Plus, I don't charge much."

He didn't. If children offered nickels or dimes or quarters, he accepted them. He also took candy bars, colorful rocks, and lucky pieces of string as payments.

"How do you live?" asked Darius, "Don't you need more money?"

"I made money in another life," Daedalus answered. "Then I found this one more interesting."

You may have noticed that Daedalus often spoke cryptically. When I say this, I mean that he spoke in short, mysterious phrases so that Darius had to guess at their meaning. Daedalus, like many adults, kept much of his life hidden. Darius had detected—beneath the joking and joyful good spirits—a sad undercurrent that seemed to run through Daedalus's life like a long, sorrowful song. He wondered if it had to do with the red bike with the twisted wheel in the basement.

For his part, Daedalus never asked Darius about his family or pried into what had happened to Darius before they met. Like Ms. Bickerstaff in the library, Daedalus seemed content just to be with Darius and help him, which is a rare thing indeed in the world of grown-ups.

Once he understood how a bike worked, Darius was able to tackle more challenging jobs. Now and then, Daedalus paid him a little extra for difficult repairs, and Darius hid the money away in case he needed it during his escape from Aunt Inga.

But it wasn't making money that interested Darius. He quickly learned that there is nothing like lending a hand to someone else to help you forget your own troubles. Many of the problems that children had with their bikes—flat tires, chains that had fallen off their sprockets, loose handlebars—were easily repaired. It gave him a wonderful feeling to give a kid back a bike that was running as good as new.

"You're a genius," a little girl said to him one morning after he had oiled her squeaky chain.

"Not really," said Darius. "Almost anybody can fix a bike."

"Not like you," she said.

"Oh, Daedalus is much better than I am," he said.

"Are you Daedalus's grandson?"

"No," said Darius. "I wish I was, but I'm not."

"You're so lucky to work with him!" said the girl. "Do you live here?"

"No, I just help."

"You're still lucky," she said. "Thanks."

"You're welcome," Darius said with a big smile.

11
Crash Landing

Darius did not do the one thing that Daedalus had asked of
him: he did not tell Aunt Inga about his trips to
Daedalus's workshop every morning. He wanted to,
because the old man had insisted. But the subject never came up
again, and Darius didn't see any point in volunteering the information to his aunt. You and I both know that kids should do
what their elders say. We know that adults are usually wiser than
kids. But I don't think you can really blame Darius for not telling
the whole truth this time. Not to Aunt Inga.

All the days that Darius was rebuilding his bicycle, Aunt Inga
never once woke up before ten o'clock. Darius always arrived
home a quarter of an hour before she got up. Darius knew how
lucky he was to have this time free. Sometimes he wondered
what would happen if Aunt Inga rose early one day and noticed
that he was missing. But he decided to worry about that when
the time came.

Still, even though he spent the early mornings with Daedalus
and some of each afternoon at the library, there were hours and
hours of the day that needed to be filled. You can really only spend
so much time by yourself before it begins to drive you crazy.

Darius could think of many things he would like to do rather than sit alone in the basement at Aunt Inga's.

He would have preferred to travel with his father to Borneo.

Or to throw water balloons off the roof with Miss Hastings.

Or even to be in school with other kids. Imagine that.

But Darius had no power to do these things. That is the problem with being a kid—very little money and no car keys.

Sometimes he thought about how nice it would be to spend the afternoons and evenings at Daedalus's house. But his friend had made it clear—the afternoon was his time to think. Darius couldn't imagine anyone doing nothing but thinking all afternoon every day, but he was sure that if anyone could do it, Daedalus could.

Since the unpleasant incident with Anthony, Darius had done his best to avoid him. But Anthony was the only other person around who was anywhere near his age. Every day Darius could hear him outside, yelling and riding his bike back and forth over the ramp he had made in the middle of the street. It always sounded like he was having a great time. Finally, one day, Darius couldn't stand it any longer.

He walked out to the street and watched Anthony ride over the ramp time and time again.

"Too bad you don't have a bike," said Anthony for the millionth time. "You could fly like me, except not as well."

Why does he have to make everything into a contest? Darius wondered. Darius was sick of Anthony's bragging, but he bit his tongue. Even though he knew that Anthony's ordinary bike and puny jumps were nothing compared to what he had seen, Darius didn't say a word. He didn't want to tell Anthony about Daedalus and his wonderful workshop, and he certainly didn't want this bully to know that he'd seen a bike that really flew. Still, the urge grew; he really wanted to ride Anthony's bike just once.

Darius stepped off the curb just as the teenager came by. "Hey, Anthony," he said.

The boy ignored him as he rode past; he pedaled faster and flew over the ramp.

"Hey, Anthony," Darius called out. "Good jump. Could I try your bike?"

Anthony slammed on the brakes and skidded to a stop in front of Darius. "What do you want? Did you say something?"

"Could I try your bike, for just a minute?"

Anthony screwed up his eyes, squinting at Darius. "What'll you give me?"

"Give you?" said Darius. "What do you want? I don't have anything."

A sly smile spread across Anthony's face. "I've got an idea. You could do something for me." The words hung in the air.

"What?" asked Darius, afraid to find out.

"You could lie down just at the end of the ramp, and I could jump over you on the bike, like at a circus or something."

This sounded like a crazy and stupid idea to Darius. "Lie down?" he said. "What if you run over me?"

"You won't get hurt. I've seen people do it all the time. I'll fly right over you."

Darius frowned. This wasn't just crazy; it was a *terrible* idea.

"Suit yourself," said Anthony. He pushed off on his bike, pedaling down the street, getting ready for another trip over the ramp.

"Okay!" Darius shouted. "I'll do it." He knew it was ridiculous, but Darius was desperate to ride the bike.

Anthony circled back. "Okay," he said, "I'll let you try it. But you've got to let me do it five times."

"You said once!" Darius protested.

"No. I didn't say how many times, and it's my bike. Five times or nothing."

What could Darius do? He thought about walking away, about going back down into the basement and spending the rest of the afternoon on his cot. But now he was already in the middle of this stupid game. "Okay," he said, "but just five."

"Sure," said Anthony. "Go lie down by the ramp."

Darius stretched out on the pavement. Anthony picked up a stick from the side of the street and handed it to Darius. "As soon as I touch down, put this stick where my back tire landed so I can see how far I went."

"Okay," said Darius, "but just those five times."

"Yeah, right," said Anthony.

When you are dealing with a slippery character like Anthony, there is one sure thing: whatever he says is not what he means. If you know someone like Anthony, deep down you know it is best to avoid him. And you also know that once he draws you into one of his schemes, it is very hard to get out of it.

Darius lay helplessly on the street, face up in front of the ramp, as Anthony flew over him on the bike again and again. Each time he flew over, Darius marked the landing place with the stick. After the fifth time, Darius sat up. "Okay, all done. Now it's my turn."

"Just a couple more," said Anthony.

"You said five," said Darius.

"Come on, don't be a chicken. Just a couple more. Let me try and beat my record."

"No. That's not fair."

"Then forget about riding the bike."

Again, what could Darius do? It was Anthony's bike and Anthony's ramp. Darius gave in and lay back down by the ramp.

Anthony took half a dozen more turns, yelling "One more time!" on every jump.

Finally, Darius stood up. "That's enough. I kept my end of the bargain. Now I get to ride."

"All right, worm," said Anthony, "if you have to have your way. But you've got to jump the ramp."

"I just want to ride."

"You have to ride over the ramp at least once," said Anthony. "I'll lie in front of it. See if you can go past where the stick is. You'll never beat me."

"You don't need to lie down," said Darius. "All I want to do is just ride your bike around the block."

But Anthony had already sprawled out on the pavement in front of the ramp.

Shrugging his shoulders, Darius climbed on the bike and pedaled down the street, then turned and headed for the ramp. The bike was big for him, but by standing on the pedals, he got it going. It was the first time he'd been on a bike in days. He couldn't help but smile. The ramp came closer and closer, and he could see Anthony lying on the other side of the ramp, his head sticking out from one side of the ramp, his feet sticking out from the other. Anthony was waving the stick in the air. Darius's heart pounded as he hit the ramp, and just as he felt the bike's wheels leave the board, he saw the stick poking up in the air, directly in front of him.

What was Anthony thinking?!

Nothing very intelligent, that's for sure.

"Nooooooo!" Darius yelled. As he passed over Anthony, the stick jammed in the spokes of the back wheel and broke. Darius lost his balance. The bike twisted wildly to one side, flying through the air sideways.

"Owwww!" Anthony screamed as the stick was wrenched from his hand. Darius tumbled off the bike, falling one way while the bike bounced and twisted in the other direction. It careened across the street and crashed into a tree. Darius hit the pavement with a thud and slid several feet along the pavement. His arm and shoulder were scraped and bleeding. He raised his head to see Anthony sitting by the ramp rubbing his wrist.

"Man," said Anthony, "that really hurt my hand."

Darius was furious. "What did you do that for?" he shouted at Anthony. "You could have killed me—and yourself, too! What's the matter with you anyway?"

Anthony wasn't even looking at him—he had gotten up and walked over to his bike by the side of the street. The handlebars were twisted to the side, and the spokes of the back wheel were bent.

"Hey, man, look what you did to my bike! It's all screwed up!"

"Me?" said Darius in disbelief. "What *I* did?"

"You were riding it," reasoned Anthony.

"You stuck the stick in it!" Darius was beside himself. "How could you do something so stupid?"

"Not that stupid. I beat you, didn't I? You didn't even come close to my mark!"

At that moment, Anthony's mother opened her front door, roused by all the yelling. She stood on her front porch with folded arms. "What's going on?" Mrs. Gritbun, asked.

Anthony didn't hesitate. "Darius was riding my bike over the ramp and messed it all up. He hurt my hand, too," he whined.

"And he didn't even do a good jump!"

I'm sure you're thinking of all sorts of things Darius could say.

You're probably hoping he'd say, "You almost got us killed, you meathead!"

Or, "Too bad your head didn't get caught in the spokes!"

Or even, "Liar, liar pants on fire!"

I wish Darius had said one of those things to Anthony. But the fact is that in situations like this, where someone says something so far from the truth, so distant from what really happened, we are often struck speechless. It's only later on that we think of absolutely brilliant things to say. Darius was so taken aback, so flabbergasted and awestruck by Anthony's ability to twist the truth for his own benefit, that he just stood there, open-mouthed.

Mrs. Gritbun waddled down the steps and out to the street. "Let me see your hand, honey," she said, reaching out to her son.

Anthony held out his paw to his mother, and she stroked it. "That's okay, Mom," he said. "I think it will be all right."

Mrs. Gritbun turned and glared at Darius, who was still standing in the street rubbing his shoulder. Then she looked back at her son. "Anthony, honey, why did you let this horrid little boy ride your bike?"

"I was just trying to be friendly," said Anthony.

This was truly an amazing statement, but Anthony said it like he meant it.

Mrs. Gritbun put her arm around her son. "Come on in, honey, and we'll put some ice on it."

"My bike is all messed up, Mom," Anthony said.

"Yes, honey, I see," said Mrs. Gritbun. "Next time your father comes home, we'll get you a new one."

Without saying anything to Darius, they headed back to their house, Anthony wheeling his ruined bike alongside him.

"YOU MADE ME FALL!" Darius finally shouted.

Mrs. Gritbun turned back on him in a fury. "You listen to me, you little troublemaker. No one made you ride over that ramp—you did it yourself. Anthony shares his things with you, and look what you do. You shouldn't have been riding his bike, anyway. You obviously don't know how to ride properly."

Anthony was standing behind his mother, making faces at Darius.

"And don't go blaming my son for something you did yourself," Mrs. Gritbun went on. "You just wait until your aunt hears about this. It's no wonder nobody wants you." She turned abruptly and walked up the steps.

"Thanks for messing everything up," Anthony said with a smirk. "And don't forget, I won."

Darius stood in the street by the ramp, rubbing his sore shoulder. He let out a sigh. He needed his own bike. Now more than ever.

12
Gertrude Gritbun's Terrible Idea

When Aunt Inga got wind of what happened, she immediately blamed Darius.

"What am I going to do with you?" she asked.

As you know, there is no right answer to this question when it comes from an angry adult.

"It wasn't my fault," Darius tried to explain. "Anthony stuck a stick in the wheel and made me fall."

"NOT YOUR FAULT? You never should have been on that bike, riding over that ramp in the first place. Don't you have a lick of sense? I knew this kind of thing would happen when I took you in. Now what are we going to do?" Aunt Inga paused and glared at him.

Darius figured this was another question that had no right answer. He kept quiet.

"Just what I thought," his aunt fumed. "You don't know what to do either. What can I say to my friend Gertrude now? You ruined her son's bike! How am I supposed to deal with that? It's good she's my friend, or she'd probably sue us, and then where would I be? Up the creek without a paddle, that's where." Aunt

Inga pulled a daintily embroidered handkerchief out of her pocket and blew her nose with a loud honk. "Well, if you're going to cause trouble like that, I'm just going to have to keep you busy around here. It's about time you earned your keep. I'll put you to work."

And she did. Aunt Inga bustled into the kitchen and came back with a bucket of water and an old toothbrush.

"Take this in the bathroom and scrub the floor with it."

"With a toothbrush?" Darius asked.

"Yes, with a toothbrush," she mimicked. "I want every tile spotless. I'm going to keep you out of mischief if it kills me, and it probably will."

Darius couldn't see how making him clean the bathroom with a toothbrush would kill her, but part of him hoped it would.

But of course it didn't.

When he'd finished with the tile floor, Aunt Inga found other mind-numbing, backbreaking jobs for Darius to do.

She had him pull dandelions out of the yard by hand. One by one, all day long.

One morning she made him dust off all her hundreds of trophies for selling magazines and arrange them in chronological order.

And, worst of all, she told him that from then on he was to go to bed in the basement at seven-thirty every night.

In the middle of summer!

It wasn't even dark yet!

Who'd ever heard of such a thing?

Darius hadn't, that's for sure.

Darius learned to survive by avoiding Aunt Inga whenever possible. After he got home from Daedalus's workshop, he'd do his chores—he couldn't believe how many dandelions could grow in one backyard—as quickly as he could. In the afternoons while she was busy with her TV programs, Darius planned his escape. At the library he studied the maps, plotting the best routes to his old town and copying them carefully in his notebook. He was a bit worried that he didn't have an address for Miss Hastings. There was no use asking Ms. Bickerstaff again about tracking her down on the computer. His old housekeeper had said she'd find a place with friends, and he had no idea who they were.

I'll just have to do some detective work when I get there, he thought. I'll ask at the stores we used to go to, and the houses in our old neighborhoods. Someone will surely know where she went.

Darius knew he would need supplies for the trip. Daedalus had already given him a kit to repair flat tires and a small can of oil for his chain. He used some of the money he had earned from repairing bikes to buy a rain poncho and a little toolkit at a surplus store not far from Daedalus's house. He'd need food, too. He thought about squirreling away some of Aunt Inga's cookies, but he was afraid she would notice. Instead, he started buying little packets of cheese and crackers from a convenience store down the street from Aunt Inga's.

He stowed all the things for his escape in his backpack and kept it under his cot. Even though it was a very small backpack, to Darius it promised another world, better than the one he lived in. It had nothing to do with his life with Aunt Inga.

But Aunt Inga was his aunt, and he couldn't avoid her all the time.

And try as he might, he couldn't always avoid Anthony. Every Tuesday and Thursday Aunt Inga would invite Mrs. Gritbun and Anthony over for a late afternoon tea, which consisted of diet cola and more cookies from the little white bags. On those occasions, Aunt Inga would give each boy a can of soda pop and two cookies and shoo them out of the living room, always reminding Darius to "entertain" Anthony. This usually meant that the boys would go outside, where Anthony would torment Darius in new and horrible ways. But when the weather was bad, they'd go into the basement, where Anthony would torture Darius until he could get away and come upstairs. That is exactly what had happened on the afternoon that Mrs. Gritbun came up with the terrible idea.

That day, Anthony had been particularly nasty. Darius had endured the usual noogies and wedgies, but when the bigger boy kneed him in the thigh, it was the last straw. Darius tore up the stairs with Anthony right behind him laughing like a hyena. The two boys burst into the living room, and Darius sat down on the floor directly across from Aunt Inga and Mrs. Gritbun, who were just finishing their soft drinks and cookies. Anthony squeezed in between his mother and Aunt Inga on the sofa.

"Having fun, boys?" asked Mrs. Gritbun.

"Yes, Mother," Anthony said, aiming an evil smile at Darius.

Darius kept quiet. What was the point of saying anything?

"They play so well," sighed Aunt Inga. "It's a pity that Anthony will have to leave for school in several weeks. I don't know what I'll do with him then."

And that was when Mrs. Gritbun uttered these horrifying words:

"*Why don't you send Darius to Crapper Academy with Anthony?*"

Darius froze. Small animals seemed to run up and down his spine and weird little insects seemed to skitter up the skin on the back of his head and over his scalp.

"Noooo...," he squeaked.

But no one heard him. Aunt Inga's eyes went from little slits to big donuts and back to slits. She began to breathe in and out in quick little bursts.

"Is that possible?" she asked as a small smile appeared on her thin and sour face. "Would there be room for him?"

"Of course," said Mrs. Gritbun. "They're always looking for new students to train."

"But isn't it very expensive?" asked Darius, searching for something that would discourage Aunt Inga.

"Oh, I'm not worried about that," said Aunt Inga excitedly. "I'll just get some more money from those Figby Migby people."

"And there are scholarships," Mrs. Gritbun enthused. "Students can work off the fee on the weekends and in the evenings, and between classes and drills and homework. There is always work to be done." She smiled at Anthony. "Wouldn't you like your playmate to come to Crapper, Anthony?"

"I think it would be just great," Anthony said, leering at Darius like a poisonous snake. If he'd had a forked tongue, it would have flickered.

"We should look into this immediately," said Aunt Inga. "I certainly can't have him underfoot for the whole school year. I'd never get anything done."

She looked at Darius.

Mrs. Gritbun looked at Darius.

Anthony looked at Darius.

They were all looking at Darius.

"I think it would be good for you, Darius," said his aunt.

Darius couldn't help himself. The words jumped out of his mouth like angry grasshoppers. "I don't want to go to Crapper! I'd hate it there!"

There was a moment of silence as the three people on the sofa stared at him. Then their mouths opened and they began to speak all at once. To Darius, they looked like the mythological three-headed monster Daedalus had told him about—Cerberus, the three-headed dog that guarded the entrance to the under-world.

Darius couldn't tell which words were coming from which mouth, they came at him so fast.

"Of all the..."

"I don't believe..."

"Why you little..."

"Horrid..."

"Ungrateful..."

"Selfish..."

"Little..."

"Brat..."

"GO TO YOUR ROOM!" (Darius knew that those words were spoken by Aunt Inga.)

"I don't even have a room!" shouted Darius. "All I have is a cot in a dark, damp basement!" Tears were running down his face, but he didn't care.

"I knew it," screeched Aunt Inga. "I just knew it would come to this." Cookie crumbs sprayed from her mouth as she spoke. "Well, just listen to me, Mr. Snootypants, you're lucky to have that much. But you won't have it for long. Nosiree Bob, you won't. I won't have you here underfoot all winter, and if the fine school that Anthony goes to will have you, it's probably the last place on earth that will."

"Miss Hastings would take me!" said Darius. "Let's find her. She would take me."

"What could she do for you?" Aunt Inga sputtered. "She's an old woman."

"She loves me!"

"GO TO YOUR ROOM!" Aunt Inga repeated, shaking with rage.

"My dungeon, you mean!" said Darius, wiping his tears. He got up and walked out of the room, leaving the hissing, seething three-headed monster muttering to itself. As he reached the stairs, he put his hand in his pocket and found Miss Hastings's silver wings. He pulled them out and held them in his fingers, rubbing them as if that would bring them to life and lift him up, away from Aunt Inga's house, and high into the sky. "I'm finishing my bike," he said out loud. "I'm coming, Miss Hastings."

But it wasn't going to be that easy.

Darius Tells His Story 13

The next morning, Darius was at Daedalus's house earlier than ever before. He rapped on the back door and it opened a crack.

Daedalus peeped out, his hair twisted and standing straight up. "What do you seek, Master Darius?" he said, squinting his eyes. "And why do you come so early to the land of the dead?"

"This isn't funny, Daedalus. You have to let me in so we can work on my bike."

"This is no way to speak to Charon, the ferryman."

"Who?"

Daedalus rolled his eyes. "Don't you remember? We talked about him. Charon, who carries people over the River Styx to the land of the dead. They put coins under their tongues to pay him. Do you have some money for me? Let me look under your tongue."

"Daedalus!" Darius sputtered. "This is no time for stories! Please let me in!"

"No one crosses the River Styx without payment...What about cinnamon buns?"

"DAEDALUS!" yelled Darius. "Let me in!"

"Okay, okay, don't be so touchy—you're acting like a grown-up," Daedalus grumbled as he opened the door. "What's the problem? Would you like some juice?"

"I don't have time to sit down and eat," said Darius. "We have to finish my bike today. It's already taken too long." He scooted down the stairs.

"What's the hurry?" Daedalus called as he followed Darius down to the workshop.

"Mrs. Gritbun had a terrible idea and now my aunt is sending me to military school and I'll be eaten alive," Darius spoke in a rush. "Anthony is already figuring out more ways to torture me. They'll stick me in Crapper and I'll never get out. We don't have much time. We have to finish my bike so I can ride away and find—"

"Wait! Slow down. What are you talking about?"

You might find it hard to believe that during all those days of working on bikes with Daedalus, Darius had not told him anything about his problems with Anthony or his plan to escape. But it's true. They were so interested in bicycles and stories of the Greek gods that they had forgotten everything else. Daedalus hadn't pried into Darius's business away from the workshop, and Darius had been grateful. Talking about his aunt or his parents or Miss Hastings just made him feel bad.

First, Darius confessed that he hadn't told Aunt Inga about coming to the workshop.

Daedalus frowned. "You promised me you would tell her!"

"I know, I know," said Darius, "but let me tell you why I didn't. I guess we'd better sit down. This may take some time."

Daedalus pulled a wooden bench from under the work counter and took a seat. Darius sat on the other end of the bench and told his story. Tears welled up in his eyes when he told about his mother's unexpected death and his father's disappearance. His cheeks grew red with anger when he talked about Aunt Inga and Anthony. By the time he got to the part about having to go to Crapper Academy, he was walking around the small kitchen in circles, waving his arms wildly.

In fact, Darius was so upset that he didn't notice the effect his story was having on Daedalus. He didn't see the look on the old man's face when he heard the name Frobisher. He didn't hear Daedalus gasp when he learned that Darius's beloved house-keeper was named Miss Hastings. Darius didn't even see the tear Daedalus wiped from his eye.

When Darius had worn himself out raving about Anthony and Aunt Inga and Crapper Academy, he collapsed in the chair and looked over at Daedalus.

His wild-haired, wonderful friend sat across from him, covering most of his face with his large, old hands.

"See, Daedalus?" Darius said. "I have to finish my bike and get out of here. Now!"

Daedalus peered at him through his fingers, his bright blue eyes now filled with tears. "I should have known right away," he said.

"What? Known what?" asked Darius.

"Your father was named Rudy?"

"Yes. How do you know?"

"And your Miss Hastings—"

"Our housekeeper."

"Gracie?"

"Yes, her first name is Grace. How did—?"

"Incredible," Daedalus murmured. "Inconceivable. But of course..." The old man cleared his throat and looked up through the basement window, high on the wall.

"How did you know them?" Darius repeated. He had the feeling something important was about to happen, but he didn't know what it was. Something was knocking on the door of his brain, but he couldn't find the doorknob to open it.

"I...um...knew Miss Hastings very well...once," Daedalus stammered.

"How did you know her?"

"We were friends."

"Wait. Wait! You were friends with Miss Hastings? Good friends?"

"You could say that."

"Wait...Daedalus. Was it you? Were you going to marry Miss Hastings a long time ago?"

Daedalus's breath caught. "Yes, it was I."

"And you knew my dad?"

"Yes," said Daedalus, frowning.

Darius didn't notice the worried look on his friend's face. He was beside himself with glee. "That's great!" he shouted. "We can find her together!" Darius didn't say it, but he was also thinking that the three of them might search for his father, too. Finally, it seemed that things were headed in the right direction.

You are probably thinking so, too. I know I am.

But then, Daedalus shook his head. "No thanks, I don't think so."

"What do you mean? What's wrong?"

"This is all happening too fast."

"Too fast for what? What do you mean? Why wouldn't you want to see her?"

"I doubt that she would want to see me. The last time I saw her she was angry with me, and I bet she still is. She was always very stubborn."

"You're wrong. She would want to see you! She needs you!"

"No, Darius, I don't think so."

"You've got to come with me. You've got to help me find her. I have to get away!"

Daedalus sighed and thought for a moment. "I will help you finish your bicycle. If you want to find Gracie...er...Miss Hastings, that's your business. But I won't go myself. It is too late for that."

"But why? Why won't you? Why don't you want to see her?"

"After everything that has happened, she would want to see me even less."

"You're wrong!"

"I'm right. I'm sure of it. Something very terrible happened between Gracie—Miss Hastings—and me. More terrible than I even knew, until now."

"But—"

"ENOUGH!" Daedalus boomed. The metal rims hanging over his head buzzed and rattled in sympathy. "I can't talk about it. No buts. No ifs. No ands."

Darius gulped, surprised at Daedalus's yelling. He had never raised his voice like that before. Darius looked closely at him. This man was different from the person he had come to know over the past several weeks. He saw a terrible unhappiness that he couldn't, for all of his eleven years, understand.

"Okay," Darius said, "but you will help me finish my bike?"

"Yes, I'll help you do that," answered Daedalus.

"Maybe we could repair the flying bike instead, since that way I could get to Miss Hastings faster?"

"No," said Daedalus. "Definitely not."

Even though Darius knew he was pushing his luck, he risked another question. "How'd you do it?"

"Do what?"

"How did you build a flying bicycle?"

"Science. I was a scientist."

"But why—"

"No!" Daedalus interrupted. *"Don't* ask me again!"

"Okay," said Darius, now close to tears. "Don't yell."

"I will help you finish your bike. But do not ask me again about the flying bike."

"Okay," Darius said. "Okay. But what about Miss Hastings?"

"No! Nothing about Gra—" He caught himself. "Nothing about Miss Hastings. Don't bring her up again." Daedalus took a deep breath and squared his shoulders. "All right," he said. "Time to finish up the spokes. And then you need to go."

Darius desperately wanted to ask more, to talk more, but he understood that the time was not right. He would have to wait.

And so will you.

A Visit from the Colonel

14

The next day, as Darius was on his way out the door to the library, he heard his aunt talking on the phone. He peeked into the living room.

"Yes, Colonel," Aunt Inga said with sugary politeness. "Yes sir, we'll look forward to seeing you. I must tell you, he's not very well behaved.... It doesn't? You can fix that? Wonderful. When does school begin?... That soon? Fine. Darius and I will look forward to meeting you.... Yes, thank you ever so much. Good-bye, Colonel Crimper."

She hung up the phone and turned to Darius. "That was the headmaster of Crapper Academy," she warbled. "What a wonderful man. So distinguished sounding. He has an opening for you at the school, and he will be coming to meet us tomorrow. I just hope you don't ruin the whole thing."

"But Aunt Inga," pleaded Darius, "I *really* don't want to go. I don't want to go to Crapper Academy. I don't want to go with Anthony. Please don't—"

"Oh, now you're singing a different tune. I just knew it. Now that I've made arrangements, you've changed your mind and you like it here? Well, it's too late for that. What's done is done."

"But—"

"I'm not in the mood for your excuses." The words spewed out of her mouth. "Don't you ever think of anyone else? You've been under the impression that the whole world is here to serve you. I guess now you'll finally find out how the world works. School starts in a week and then I'll be free of you."

Darius glared at his aunt.

"I know you don't like me," she said. "This will be best for both of us. You won't have to see me except at Christmas and in the summer—unless they have a summer program."

At precisely eleven o'clock the next morning, there was a sharp knock on the front door.

"Answer that!" shouted Aunt Inga from her bedroom. "I'm not quite ready yet."

Darius opened the door. A very large, round man dressed in an olive-green military uniform stood before him.

"Atten-hut!" the man shouted.

Darius was so stunned he couldn't speak. All he could do was stare. Everything about the man was massive. The head on top of his rotund body was big and square. He had enormous features—large ears, a bulbous nose, a huge mouth with puffy lips, and the bushiest eyebrows Darius had ever seen.

"Atten-hut!" the man bellowed. Still Darius stared.

The man ripped open the screen door and leaned over until his bushy eyebrows and monstrous mouth were inches from Darius's face.

"Excuse me, son," he said in a menacing whisper, "but maybe you're hard of hearing. I said...ATTEN-HUT!" The roar hit

Darius like a freight train and he jumped back two feet. Before he knew what he was doing, he found himself standing straight with his arms at his sides.

A smile spread across the colonel's face. "That's better, son. You must be Darius. I've come to meet you and your wonderful aunt."

"Here I am," sang out Aunt Inga as she came into the living room all dressed up in a horrible frilly dress that Darius had never seen. "You must be Colonel Crimper." Her voice was as cheery and sunny as a kindergarten teacher on the first day of school. Darius felt like throwing up. He'd never heard Aunt Inga use that voice before, and he instantly spotted it as a fake. He noticed that it didn't bother the colonel at all.

Darius knew that was a bad sign. Anyone who couldn't tell Aunt Inga was being fake was probably fake himself. Or a monster that didn't give a fig.

Aunt Inga ordered Darius to sit on the most uncomfortable chair in the living room and listen while she and Colonel Crimper talked. Aunt Inga said the most terrible and untrue things about Darius, as if he weren't even in the room. Colonel Crimper nodded sympathetically and assured her that his academy had very effective methods for dealing with unruly lads.

Darius had often heard his father say that going from a bad situation to a worse one was like "leaping from the frying pan into the fire." That expression now had a whole new meaning for Darius. If Aunt Inga was a frying pan, Colonel Crimper was a fire. A big one.

"Of course, our students are still boys," said Colonel Crimper as they opened the second bag of cookies, "but we believe it's never too early to start them on the road to manhood. We don't coddle them. Talking in class is not tolerated; on the third offense the student is put in solitary confinement for three days. They can talk as much as they want there!" The colonel laughed at his own joke.

"You put them in jail for talking?" Darius blurted out.

Both Aunt Inga and Colonel Crimper stared at him. Neither of them spoke.

"I was just curious," Darius muttered.

To make matters worse, halfway through the visit Mrs. Gritbun and Anthony showed up. Aunt Inga's singsong voice may have made Darius feel sick, but Anthony's behavior was enough to make him throw up everything he had ever eaten.

"Good morning, Colonel Crimper, SIR!" shouted Anthony, standing at attention, staring off into space and saluting.

The colonel rose and saluted back.

"At ease, Gritbun, at ease." The colonel chuckled. "Gritbun, Gritbun, Gritbun. One of our very best. A man we're proud of. Isn't that right, Gritbun?"

"Yes SIR!" shouted Anthony.

Darius felt his undigested breakfast rising up in his throat.

"This is the kind of young man Crapper produces!" the colonel boomed. With the larger audience, he raised his voice and went on and on about the wonders of Crapper Academy. The two ladies enjoyed his blather as much as he enjoyed blathering.

The colonel blabbed. Aunt Inga and Mrs. Gritbun smiled. Anthony smirked. Darius stared at the ceiling. After another half hour of bluster and bombast, Colonel Crimper got up to leave. At the door he said to Aunt Inga, "I'm quite confident everything will work out fine. Anthony Gritbun is one of our finest cadets. And I'll make sure he personally sees young Darius through the first term. You'll do that, won't you, Gritbun?"

Anthony directed one of his most evil smiles at Darius.

"Yes, sir!" Anthony said with great relish.

Why can't anyone else see how terrible he is? thought Darius.

"You are all so kind," said Aunt Inga. "How can we thank you? Finally, finally, something is going right. It's about time, after all I've been through."

"It's nothing," said the colonel, "just doing my job...but, if you'd excuse us, I'd like young Darius to walk me to the car, so we might have a word in private—a little talk between men, you understand."

"Of course, of course," giggled Aunt Inga. "You go on ahead."

Colonel Crimper grabbed Darius by the arm and led him down the porch stairs to the street. When they reached the car, he turned and bent over Darius, glowering.

"Listen, you little heathen," he hissed, "I've seen your kind—I know what you're like. And I know what to do with you. I know how to straighten you out."

Darius's mouth went dry and his legs wobbled.

"I'll make you a new man, whether you want to be one or not. I can hardly wait."

Darius thought he might faint.

"What do you have to say to that?" the colonel rumbled, leaning even closer.

"I...I...," squeaked Darius.

"Speak up, boy, and call me 'sir'!"

I know what you are thinking.

You are wishing that Darius would say, "No way, you big lunk!"

Or, "Not for a million dollars. Not for a trillion dollars!"

Or maybe you are wishing that Darius would just throw up on Colonel Crimper's shoes. That would be very satisfying.

But you know that speaking up to loud, bossy adults is a very difficult thing to do. Even when they are mean and wrong.

Instead, Darius looked down at his own shoes and said, "Yes sir."

But inside his head Darius was saying, *No, no, no!*

Back in Daedalus's basement, Darius tried to concentrate. It bothered him that his friend had been so quiet since their argument about Miss Hastings. Daedalus answered his questions and gave a hand when he needed help, but most of the time he busied himself on other projects and left Darius to work alone.

Forcing all other thoughts out of his head, Darius buckled down to the job at hand. He was in a hurry—there is nothing like a deadline to make you finish something, and escaping Crapper Academy was about the best motivation he'd ever had. Over the next two days, he reassembled the bike.

He greased the cups that held the ball bearings, put the bearings back in each cup, and reassembled both wheels.

He put together the headset that held the handlebars.

He cleaned and greased the chain and checked each link to make sure it was strong.

Then, placing the bike frame upside down on the worktable, Darius attached the wheels and gave them a whirl.

They spun and spun and spun. There in Daedalus's basement, it seemed they would spin on forever.

"Daedalus," he called, "I think it's finished."

Together they stood back and looked at their handiwork. The chrome glistened, the black chain stood out against the silver wheels and sprocket, and the brilliant blue-green of the frame and fenders sparkled and shone.

"What do you think of it, Daedalus?"

"It's beautiful," said Daedalus. "You did a wonderful job."

"With your help."

"Not much of that," said Daedalus. "Are you ready for the first ride?"

"I sure am," Darius said.

They carried the bicycle up the stairs, out the back door, through the maze of bikes and bike parts, around the house, and into the street. Darius climbed on the bike.

"Wait! Wait!" Daedalus yelled. "No helmet! You have to have a helmet." The old man disappeared into the house and returned with a scratched-up football helmet. He strapped it on Darius's head.

"You have to promise me you'll always wear a helmet," Daedalus said.

"I promise," said Darius.

"And you'll be very careful."

"Sure."

"No riding at night."

"Right."

"No riding against the traffic."

"Okay, okay, Daedalus. I know all that."

"*I mean it!*" said Daedalus, sounding very upset.

"All right," said Darius. "I promise I'll be really, really careful." He looked up at the old man.

"Now," said Daedalus, finally satisfied, "you must christen the bicycle. What do you want to name it?"

Darius thought hard. He wanted to find just the right name. A shaft of early morning sunlight struck the bike and seemed to set it aglow. The handlebars sparkled and the shiny blue-green frame gleamed. Darius remembered the story about the god who pulled the sun's chariot across the sky. Apollo.

"Apollo," said Darius. "The bike will be Apollo One."

Daedalus's face broke into a little smile. "Fine, Apollo it is then. Ready for liftoff. All systems go." He stepped back.

When Darius stood up and pushed down on the pedal, the bike moved forward into the street, seemingly on its own. The sprockets whirred and clicked. Darius watched the front wheel spin over the pavement. He reached the end of the street in no time, wheeled around, and headed back. He zoomed by Daedalus, rang the bell once, and turned down the street again. The bike rode like a dream. He circled by Daedalus again, picking up speed.

"Yeeeeehaaaaah!" Darius whooped.

"Be careful!" yelled Daedalus.

Darius rode the bike round and round until it was time to leave. He said good-bye to Daedalus and pedaled toward Aunt Inga's house. His plan was in action—he was going to escape!

Just as he rounded the last corner, he glanced at his watch. It was nine-thirty, half an hour before Aunt Inga would get up. He took one more spin around the block, then pulled into the driveway and hopped off his bike. Humming quietly to himself, he wheeled the bike to the back door and reached for the doorknob.

"Good morning," a grim voice spoke. Darius jumped. He

looked up to see Aunt Inga standing on the other side of the screen door in her bathrobe.

Her mouth was locked in a gruesome smile.

Her hair, sticking out from her head like a nest of angry snakes, was a frightful mess.

She looked like Medusa in a very bad mood.

15

Remember, You Can Fly

"Aunt Inga," Darius said. He forced his lips up into a weak smile. His stomach flipped over and over like a ride at an amusement park. "What are you doing up so early?" he asked as innocently as he could.

"Where have you been?" she demanded.

"Um, just out. Out for a ride," Darius answered, immediately regretting his choice of words. Aunt Inga was upset, but she hadn't noticed the bicycle yet.

Now she did.

"Where did you get that bicycle?" she asked.

"This one?" asked Darius.

"No, the bicycle in the tree. Yes, of course I mean *that* one!" Aunt Inga peered at the shiny frame and the new wheels. "Hmmm," she said. "It looks familiar."

"Um, yeah," mumbled Darius.

"Where did you get it?"

Right now you are probably hoping that Darius will say, "I found it in the street!"

Or, "I bought it with my inheritance."

Or, "TAKE A GUESS! THERE'S A PRIZE IF YOU GUESS RIGHT!"

But he didn't. Darius was too flustered to tell a lie or make a joke.

"I...uh...it was...uh...in the basement," he stammered.

Aunt Inga's bottom lip began to quiver, and her top lip lifted so Darius could see her teeth.

Uh oh, he thought.

"That bicycle is mine!" she hissed.

"I wondered whose it was," said Darius.

"What...are...you...doing...with...that...bicycle?" Aunt Inga spit out each word as if it were a pit from a rotten prune.

"Riding it," said Darius. He didn't mean it to be a smart-aleck answer; he was saying as little as he possibly could, trying to stay out of trouble. But as soon as he said those words, he knew they would only make Aunt Inga madder.

"That's my bicycle!" she screamed. "YOU'VE STOLEN MY BICYCLE!"

"Aunt Inga, I didn't steal it. I was only borrowing it. I didn't know it was yours. No one was using it. Look. I fixed it up and—"

"You stole it! You took it without asking. I just knew it. I just knew you would do something like this. Now leave it right there and go to your room!"

"I'm sorry, Aunt Inga. Please let me keep the bicycle."

"Do as I say. Right now."

Darius's head drooped. Aunt Inga opened the door, and Darius walked down into the basement. He lay there on his cot for the longest time, thinking of all the hours he had wasted, all his plans that had come to nothing. He stared at the ceiling of the basement, looking at the cobwebs hanging from the floor-boards.

Late that afternoon, Darius dared to creep upstairs. He looked out the door. The bike was not there. Heart beating wildly, he went into the living room. As usual, his aunt was watching television.

"Aunt Inga," he said, "where's the bicycle?"

"You can forget about the bicycle. It's gone. I gave it to Anthony, since you ruined his." Without taking her eyes off the television screen, she grabbed a handful of cookies from the bag on her lap and stuffed them into her mouth.

Too stunned to respond, Darius left the room and headed toward the basement. When he came to the steps, though, he stopped. As quietly as possible, he slid out the back door and closed it silently behind him. He paused to listen. All he could hear was the television blaring from the living room. No sounds of Anthony in the street, jumping the ramp and shouting. As Darius scurried down the driveway, he almost collided with the mailman.

"Hello, there, fella," said the mailman. "You live here, right?"

"Yes sir," said Darius.

"Why don't you just take these letters up the walk for me, then?"

Before Darius had a chance to answer, the mail carrier handed the letters to him and hurried on down the street. Intending to slip the letters in the mailbox and get away before Aunt Inga heard anything, Darius tiptoed up the porch steps. Just as he was about to put the mail in the box by the door, he noticed the small envelope on top. It was addressed to him. He recognized the handwriting.

"Miss Hastings!" he whispered to himself.

Her address was on the envelope. Now he knew exactly where she lived. He put the letter in his pocket, slipped the other mail in the box, and closed the lid quietly. After looking both ways to make sure no one was in sight, Darius took off down the street. Several blocks away, he stopped and pulled out the envelope. Fingers trembling, he tore it open and read the letter:

Dear Darius,

I hope that you are well and feeling more comfortable in your new home. I am writing this to you, even though I am beginning to think you are not getting my letters. Or maybe you are just very busy in your new home.

I should not be so curious about how you are getting along, but I am. If I don't hear from you soon, I will try to contact someone who I think lives near you. I have not spoken with the person for a long time, but I think if I asked, he might check up on you for me. I will try and find his address or phone number. His name is Daedalus Panforth, just so you know if he does show up.

I am getting along.

I think of you every day.

Your friend,
Grace Hastings

Darius stuffed the letter back in his pocket and began to run. Tears stung his eyes and his chest heaved as he ran, closer and closer to Daedalus's house.

He did not see Anthony following behind him, pedaling slowly on a beautiful, bright blue-green bike.

Darius burst into Daedalus's house without knocking. He knew that he shouldn't disturb his friend while he was thinking, but this was an emergency.

"Daedalus!" Darius yelled. He stopped short. Taped on every wall of the living room were large sheets of paper covered with mathematical equations—numbers, symbols, lines, squiggles—like some alien language.

"Hmmmm?" said a voice from the corner. Darius whirled around. There was Daedalus stretched out on the couch, an open book lying over his face.

"Daedalus? Are you sleeping?"

The old man lifted the book and peeped out. "What? Who?"

"What are you doing?" asked Darius. "You told me you thought during the afternoon."

"I do," said Daedalus, struggling to sit up on the couch.

"It looked more like sleeping to me," said Darius.

"Close, but not the same. When you sleep, your mind takes you where it wants to go. When you think, you take your mind where you want to go. But what are you doing here? Why aren't you at home, being eaten alive?"

"I have been eaten alive," Darius wailed. "Aunt Inga got up early! She saw me with the bike and said I stole it from her."

"You stole your Aunt Inga's bike?" Daedalus seemed groggy, like he was still sleeping. Or thinking.

"No! My bike! The bike we fixed. She took it away from me and gave it to Anthony! Daedalus, what will I do now? Everything is hopeless. I'll never get there now. I've got to have a new bike!" Darius rushed to the basement door and charged down the stairs.

Daedalus got up slowly and followed Darius down to the workshop. "What are you doing?" he asked.

"If you won't help me, I'll do it myself. I'll build another bike."

"And where were you going?"

"You know! To Miss Hastings—she'll know what to do."

Daedalus sat down on the bottom step. He leaned over, resting his arms on his knees.

"I can't give up now, Daedalus," moaned Darius. "They're coming to get me tomorrow. They'll take me away to that horrible school. No one will ever see me again!"

Daedalus was silent. Darius waited for him to say something. Why didn't he speak? Why wouldn't he help?

With no sign of help from the old man, Darius started gathering bicycle parts on his own. He quickly found a pair of handlebars and two rims that seemed to be in good shape and placed them on the workbench. The picture on the wall above the bench top caught his eye. It was the drawing of the boy on the bicycle, flying in the air.

"Boy," he mumbled to himself, "I could use a bike like that now."

"You're a strong boy, Darius," Daedalus said. "You can survive that silly school."

"I don't want to just survive! I want to live! I want to find Miss Hastings! If I only had one of your flying bicycles, I could get away."

Daedalus still didn't answer.

"What's wrong, Daedalus? Why won't you help me fly?" Darius sank down to the floor. The world seemed to be falling in on top of him, and there was no way he could escape. Even Daedalus, the person he trusted most, didn't seem to care.

It was the last straw. Darius felt very alone.

Suddenly, he saw his father quite clearly in his mind. He missed him terribly. He always missed him, but now he needed him more than ever. In spite of himself, he began to cry. He couldn't stop. He cried and cried.

While he sobbed, he felt Daedalus sit next to him on the floor. Finally, Darius's tears were all cried out. "There's no hope left," he whispered, trying to catch his breath.

And then Daedalus spoke.

"Darius," he said, "I have something to tell you."

Darius wiped his nose on his sleeve and looked up. It seemed that the old man was trying to find the right words.

"When he was a boy, your father Rudy used to come into my shop and watch me work, just like you do. In fact, I was the one who taught him to ride his first two-wheeler." Daedalus smiled briefly at the memory, then turned serious again. "In those days I had ideas about the way the universe worked. I used bicycles to test my theories. Someone else might have used rockets, or sub-atomic particles. But bicycles are cheaper and more available. I invented all sorts of devices to improve their performance. And one day, I hit on a discovery that surprised even me."

"A bike that could fly?" asked Darius.

"Yes," said Daedalus. "I added another gear, a sixth one, that changed its physics. And it worked. The bike didn't respond to the law of gravity. It flew! Even though I had intended to keep it a secret, your father found out about it. He was about eleven."

"I'm eleven," said Darius.

"I know," Daedalus said. "Your father was a little full of himself in those days. He had a tremendous amount of energy."

"That's my dad," Darius agreed.

"Yes." Daedalus nodded. "He begged and begged to try the bike out. For a long time, I refused. Finally, though, he pestered me until I gave in and designed a smaller version, one just his size."

"The bike in the picture!"

"Yes. But when Gracie—Miss Hastings—found out, she was furious with me. I thought I could make it safe. She said that it didn't matter, that I should destroy the plans and get rid of the bikes. I didn't listen, though. I was too excited about my discovery. I kept working on them, trying to perfect them. My calculations were correct for a large bike, but there was something wrong with the smaller one—because of the difference in mass, in weight."

Daedalus closed his eyes for a moment. He seemed to be collecting his thoughts. "Now, after all these years, I think I finally understand the adjustments I should have made. But at the time I didn't know. And one day..." Daedalus paused and blew air out through his mouth.

"Go ahead, Daedalus," Darius said, touching the old man's arm. "Please tell me."

"One day, when I wasn't there, Rudy took the bike from my shop. I had warned him not to ride without me, but I suppose you can't blame him. He managed to get it into the air—but he was too young and too eager, and the bike wasn't ready. The mechanics and the physics of the bike were wrong. He lost his balance, and he fell."

"From up in the air?" Darius asked.

Daedalus nodded grimly.

"Wait," said Darius, putting the pieces of the puzzle together. "That's the red bike I found back in the corner! That's why the wheel is bent. My dad wrecked the bike when he fell out of the sky!"

"He was only fifteen or twenty feet up in the air," said Daedalus. "But it was terrible. He broke his leg in two places."

Darius thought of his dad's hiccupping walk. "That's why my dad limped," he whispered.

"Yes, and it was my fault." Daedalus took out a handkerchief and wiped his forehead. "I felt terrible about the accident. I went to see Rudy in the hospital, but Gracie wouldn't let me in the room. She loved your father more than anything in the world, you know. I loved both of them, and I had let both of them down."

"You didn't do it on purpose."

"Not on purpose. But I did it. I was wrong. Gracie was right. She almost lost her job, too, because of the accident. There was nothing I could do. We argued. I was as upset as she was. I didn't blame her when she stopped speaking to me."

"But you still could have gotten along," Darius insisted. "She still thinks about you. I know she does."

Daedalus shook his head. "Not long after the accident, I changed jobs and moved here. I never heard from Gracie again. I hid the plans for the flying bicycles away and buried myself in other work. And now your father is gone, and I feel responsible. If I hadn't taught him how to ride the bike, or talked so much about flying, he might not have disappeared."

"A hot air balloon is different from a bicycle."

"It wasn't the bicycle," Daedalus said. "It was the flying. If you want to fly, you have to be ready. You have to know your possibilities, true, but you also have to know your limits. Sometimes when you fly, you forget who you are. You're alone, and you forget. I know that now. It's very exciting to try new things, but you can never forget who you are. When you're learning to fly, you first need a safe place to fall. I should have given that safe place to your father. I didn't. That was my fault."

"It's not the same with me," said Darius. "You can show me the right way."

"I can't take a chance on another accident. I'd never get over it if something terrible happened to you."

"Don't you see? Something terrible *is* going to happen to me if you don't help. We can still find Miss Hastings. We have to!"

"She doesn't want to see me. And we don't even know where she—"

"Yes, she does," Darius interrupted. "Yes, we do. Look!" He pulled out the letter and handed it to Daedalus.

The old man read the letter, then folded the paper with trembling hands. "I don't think I can do anything about this," he said. "After all that's happened."

"Sure you can," said Darius.

"No, I can't. It's too late now." Tears welled up in Daedalus's eyes.

Darius reached in his pocket, looking for a tissue—something to dry tears and sadness. Instead, his hand wrapped around the silver wings Miss Hastings had given him. He pulled them out and held his clenched fist out to the old man.

"Look," Darius said, opening his hand to reveal the charm in his palm.

Daedalus drew in his breath. "Where did you get that?"

"Miss Hastings gave it to me. She told me what you said to her: 'Remember, you can fly!'"

"She said that?" Daedalus asked.

"Yes. Those were her exact words. Isn't that what you said to her?"

Daedalus looked off across the basement, but he might as well have been looking off into a clear blue sky with no end. He was remembering something from long ago.

"Didn't you say that?" Darius asked again.

"Yes, I did."

"Don't you see, Daedalus? She wanted me to fly, too. Do you think she would have said that if she didn't think about you? Somehow she knew that you would find me!" Darius grabbed the old man by the shoulders. "Come on, let's fix the red bike. You said you knew what was wrong. We can fly together to Miss Hastings."

Daedalus shook his head. "What if you fell?"

"You'll be with me! I'll be careful. I won't forget who I am. I trust you, Daedalus. You won't let me fall. We can do it!"

Daedalus gasped at those words—his eyes filled with tears again. And then a small, mischievous smile appeared on the old man's face. "It wouldn't be very responsible of me," he said slyly.

"You're saving my life! That's responsible," Darius said. "I'll die at Crapper Academy! Anthony will *really* eat me alive."

Daedalus glanced away, then back at Darius. The old man grinned. "All right," he said.

"Thank you!" Darius shouted, jumping up and down. "Thank you, thank you, thank you!"

"But wait! If I fix this bike, if I adjust the sixth gear, you must promise you'll be very careful."

"Okay," said Darius.

"Promise me. Say it."

"I promise."

"You have to wear a helmet!"

"Of course!"

"All right. I'll try to get it ready tonight. You come here early tomorrow morning, and we'll go find Miss Hastings. Then we'll see what we can do together."

"I love you, Daedalus," Darius said. He threw his arms around him.

The old man coughed and sputtered, "All right, all right. That's enough. Get back to your aunt's. I'll work on the bike. I just hope I'm right about the calculations."

"I'm sure you are. See you tomorrow!" Darius dashed up the stairs and out the door. Determined to reach the house before Aunt Inga realized he was gone, he raced through the streets. He didn't have a bike, but he hoped he would soon.

If Darius had looked back, he would have seen the shiny blue-green bike, still trailing him.

16
One Last Chance

When Darius made it back to the house, Aunt Inga was just finishing her magazine sales calls. During dinner, not a word was said about the bicycle or about Crapper Academy. In fact, not a word was said at all. Darius almost dared to hope that Aunt Inga had forgotten her plans to send him away.

Early the next morning, while it was still dark, Darius slipped out of bed and tiptoed up the basement stairs. When he opened the door to the hallway, the light switched on suddenly, and there, towering over him, was Aunt Inga.

"Going somewhere?" she asked.

Darius felt the world come crashing down on him again.

"No," he sighed, "just to the bathroom."

"Hah!" Her laugh rattled in her throat. "I doubt that. You were going to sneak out again. Well, not this time, bucko. I've been up all night, waiting and listening."

"Why were you doing that?"

"I know about you and Mr. Daedalus What's-his-name. I know all about it."

"Daedalus?" Darius gasped. "You know about Daedalus? How?"

"Because Anthony told me that he followed you yesterday afternoon when you went over there. He saw you go in the house, and he stayed until you came out. I know what's going on—you can't trick me anymore." Aunt Inga grabbed Darius by the arm and led him down the hall. "Go to the bathroom, but then you're going right back down to the basement to pack your bags. You'll stay there until the colonel comes to take you to the Crapper, where you belong."

"But—"

"No buts this time, mister. Nosiree Bob—it's the end of the road for you."

And it looked like it was.

When Darius came back upstairs, Aunt Inga was waiting for him at the door. She didn't take her eyes off him for a moment. She made him put his bags by the front door, ready to go when the colonel arrived. The entire time, Darius kept thinking, searching, trying to discover a way out of his predicament.

Darius thought of Daedalus and the marvelous bike waiting for him; escape and freedom seemed so close. But a flying bicycle did no good if he couldn't get near it.

It looked as if he was really going to Crapper Academy.

Shortly before noon, Anthony and Mrs. Gritbun showed up at the house with all of Anthony's belongings for school. While the two women talked to one another, Anthony taunted Darius.

"I'm taking my *new* bicycle to school. It's right outside. Would you like to see it?"

Darius tried to ignore him, but Anthony wouldn't shut up.

"A couple more hours, we'll get to school, and you'll be all mine. I'll teach you a thing or two."

Darius knew it would make Anthony madder, but he couldn't

help talking back. "You'll see," he said. "I'll never go to that stupid school. Or give in to someone as mean and stupid as you."

Anthony grabbed Darius around the neck and gave him a sharp rap on the top of his head with his knuckles.

"Ouch!" yelled Darius. "Stop it!"

"Don't let him out of your sight," called out Aunt Inga. "He doesn't know what's good for him."

And that is how things stood when Darius heard a car door slam out front. He broke loose from Anthony's grasp and looked out the window.

Colonel Crimper from Crapper Academy was getting out of a big black sedan. Darius gulped. The colonel marched up the walk, looking even bigger and meaner than before.

A loud knock announced the headmaster's arrival. Aunt Inga seized Darius by the arm and led him to the front door. Anthony followed behind them. Aunt Inga opened the door, still fiercely holding on to Darius with her other hand.

At this moment you may be wishing that a superhero would appear.

Or a wizard.

Or an enormous carnivorous caterpillar, sixty feet long, that inhaled horrid people.

Nope. Just humans in this story. Some pleasant ones. Some unpleasant ones. It's too late to bring in other creatures now.

Especially carnivorous caterpillars.

Darius was stuck.

"Good afternoon, ma'am," said Colonel Crimper. "I've come for your nephew."

"You're most welcome to him. He's all packed. You can have him now."

And then Gertrude Gritbun spoke up. "Why don't we all go outside for a picture with the colonel? So we can have a reminder of our children going off to school."

"Oh yes," said Aunt Inga, nervously patting her hair into place. "But first," she whispered to Mrs. Gritbun, "let me...um...slip on something a little nicer. I've been so busy I haven't had a chance to think about myself. It'll just take a minute." Turning to Anthony, she added, "Anthony, dearest, keep your eye on Darius for me."

"Gladly," snickered Anthony.

Aunt Inga let go of her nephew and disappeared into her bedroom.

"Don't move, worm," Anthony breathed in Darius's ear.

Mrs. Gritbun and the colonel stepped outside to look for a place to take the picture.

Darius's mind was working at full speed. Now was his chance. Now or never. He knew what he had to do.

"Hey, Anthony," he said. "Let's watch some television."

"Okay. Not a bad idea for a jerk," said Anthony, plopping down into Aunt Inga's comfortable chair.

Darius picked up the remote and clicked the set on. Someone had just won a lifetime supply of frozen onion rings on a game show. People in crazy costumes were screaming and clapping their hands together. Darius turned up the volume a notch.

His idea worked like a dream. In an instant Anthony was hypnotized by the television. He sat there, transfixed. Darius quietly tiptoed into the kitchen and slipped silently out the back door.

Darius tore through the neighbors' backyards and emerged on the sidewalk several houses up. He hid behind a shrub and looked back. Mrs. Gritbun and the colonel were standing by the big black car.

And then he took off toward Daedalus's house.

He ran like the wind.

When a commercial came on, Anthony woke up. He looked around and saw that Darius was missing.

"That stupid twerp got away! He tricked me! I'll kill him!" he ranted.

Aunt Inga came out of her bedroom half dressed, hopping on a slippered foot while she tried to put a shoe on the other. Her hair shot out of her head at odd angles.

"What?" she bellowed. "Where is he?"

"I don't know. He was here just a second ago. Maybe he's in the bathroom."

"No, he's not in the bathroom!" Aunt Inga screamed. "He got away. We have to catch him."

"I'll pound him to dust!" roared Anthony.

"I bet he went to that old guy's house, old Daedalus Hoozydunk," said Aunt Inga.

"And I know where he lives!" yelled Anthony.

"Then let's go!" sputtered Aunt Inga, hurriedly buttoning her dress.

The two of them collided in the doorway, then Aunt Inga shoved Anthony out of her way. She bustled down the walk with Anthony right behind her and quickly explained to Mrs. Gritbun and the colonel what had happened. They all piled into the big black car and took off.

When Darius reached Daedalus's house, his heart was hammering in his chest and he had to gulp for breath.

The first thing he saw was Daedalus's flying bike leaning against the porch. Extra wheels, fenders, sprockets, and handlebars sprouted from it at all angles like exotic rainforest plants.

Standing beside it was a smaller bike Darius barely recognized. It had to be his father's bike—the one he had seen under the basement stairs. Daedalus had repaired the wheel and polished the chrome to a silvery glow. He had replaced the worn seat with a shiny new black leather one and attached clean fins and wings to the frame. The body of the bike, sporting a fresh coat of red paint, sparkled in the morning sun.

"My bike," Darius said to himself as he ran his hand through the streamers dangling from the handle grips. A football helmet the same color red as the bicycle hung by its strap over one side of the handlebars. On the gear shifter Daedalus had posted a small sign:

> CAUTION: SIXTH GEAR FOR
> EMERGENCIES ONLY.
> HOLD ON TIGHT. DON'T FLY ALONE!

Darius could barely keep from jumping on the bike and riding away. Where was Daedalus anyway? Their time was running out. He ran up the porch steps and pounded on the door. No one answered.

"Daedalus! Open up! It's me! We have to go!" Darius opened the door and called out again, "Daedalus! Where are you?"

The house was silent. Darius went to the basement stairs and yelled for Daedalus. Still no answer.

Darius returned to the kitchen and stood by the table, wondering what to do.

And then he smelled it. Memories came flooding back. He couldn't believe it.

It was the distinct smell of burnt toast.

He looked at the toaster. Sticking out of it was a piece of bread, charred a dark, dark brown.

"Miss Hastings is here!" he shouted. "Miss Hastings! Miss Hastings!" he called, walking through the house again. He ran down the stairs to the basement workspace. There was no one there. Darius started up the stairs, but something made him stop. He looked back at the wall above the workbench; the picture of the boy on the bike with the balloons on each fender caught his eye. He scampered back down the steps and pulled the picture down. He peered closely at it, then turned it over.

On the back were these words:

> To Mr. Daedalus,
> Thanks.
> Love, Rudy—Your Flyboy

Darius flipped the picture back over. *Flyboy.* That's what his father always called him. He put the picture on the workbench and ran upstairs. He tried to fight off a feeling of panic. Had Daedalus and Miss Hastings gone off without him?

17
Flyboy

Darius dashed out the front door and looked down the street. His heart leapt when he saw a tandem bicycle approaching. Pedaling away on the front seat was Daedalus. Behind him, on the second seat, sat a familiar figure Darius hadn't seen for ages.

"Miss Hastings! Daedalus!" Darius waved wildly. "Miss Hastings! What are you doing here?"

His housekeeper was wearing a helmet that looked like a mushroom. She smiled nervously, but didn't raise her hand from the handlebars. "Hello, Darius! Hello!" she called out. "I came to find you. We were out looking for you!"

Daedalus rang the bell on the handlebars. *Ching ching ching!*

Darius started to run toward them, but then a terrible sight sent chills down his spine. Turning onto the street, only a few hundred yards behind Daedalus and Miss Hastings, was Colonel Crimper's big black car.

Darius's heart stuck in his throat. He was trapped. Which way to go? Daedalus's house was at the end of a dead-end street. Darius thought about trying to reach Daedalus and Miss Hastings before Colonel Crimper and the others caught up to them, but he gave up on that idea. The car was coming too fast.

If his aunt and the colonel and Anthony got ahold of him, there was no telling what they would do.

The big black sedan was cruising down the street, heading straight for him. When it passed Daedalus and Miss Hastings on their bike, the car seemed to pick up speed.

Darius had to get away. He turned and started running toward Daedalus's house.

The colonel honked the horn. Aunt Inga was hanging out the passenger side window. "Stop!" she shrieked. "Stop right now, Darius!"

"We'll get you, you pathetic worm," yelled Anthony from a back window.

Darius darted around to the side of the porch. There was the red bike, waiting for him, sparkling in the sun. He strapped on the helmet, flung himself on the seat, and started pedaling. He twisted the handlebars one way and another, making his way through the maze of bicycle parts in Daedalus's yard.

"Wait, Darius! No! Wait!" Daedalus was calling to him, but Darius was too scared to stop. He was determined not to end up at Crapper Academy. Through the jumble of bicycles, he saw an opening into an alley, and beyond it the backyards of other houses. Between the houses he saw another street. He pushed the pedals even harder, riding into the neighboring backyard.

Colonel Crimper's car screeched to a halt, skidded a few feet, and crashed into the fence in front of Daedalus's house. Bikes toppled down from the fence onto the hood of his car.

"Keep going!" screamed Aunt Inga. "He's getting away!"

"I'll get that twerp," Anthony said. He threw open the car door, almost smashing it into the tandem bike.

Daedalus swerved to avoid the door and guided the bicycle

up onto the sidewalk. He hopped off the bike and turned to Miss Hastings.

"Are you all right, Gracie?" he asked.

"My goodness, yes," she answered. "How exciting!"

"Gimme a bike, you old geezer," growled Anthony.

"I wouldn't give anything to anyone as rude as you," replied Daedalus.

"Then I'll just take one," Anthony shot back. He turned and ran through the yard, looking for a bike. "This is all junk!" he bellowed, rummaging through the dismantled bicycles. "Trash! Worthless!"

"You are as blind as a bat," said Daedalus. "These things are priceless."

"Don't say my son is blind! He can see perfectly well," Mrs. Gritbun squawked.

Aunt Inga was peering at Miss Hastings as she took off her helmet. "Haven't I met you somewhere before?" she asked.

"Yes, I am Miss Hastings. Darius's housekeeper."

"I knew it! I should have known you were behind all this!" Aunt Inga breathed heavily.

"I am behind nothing. It's about time that you realized—"

A loud whoop stopped her in midsentence.

"Finally!" Anthony roared. "Here's a bike I can use! It's pretty weird looking, but it'll do." He wheeled out Daedalus's flying bicycle, loaded down with fins and extra equipment.

"No!" pleaded Daedalus, running toward Anthony. "Not that one! It's not safe! You mustn't ride it!"

"Back off, you old fart. You just don't want me to catch the little creep!"

"Of course I don't. But this bike's not safe. And you don't have a helmet. I must ask that you not ride that bike. It's for your own good."

"Buzz off, old man," said Anthony as he turned the bike in Darius's direction and climbed on. "I'm outta here!"

"Please, no!" Daedalus ran toward Anthony, desperate to stop him.

Anthony gave Daedalus a shove and sent him sprawling back into a pile of training wheels.

Daedalus struggled to disentangle himself from the little wheels and frames. "Whatever you do, don't push it into the last gear," he shouted frantically, trying to get to his feet. "Don't use the seventh gear! You're not ready for it! Listen to me!"

"Forget you," said Anthony. He rode off, dodging a heap of handlebars, and followed Darius into the alley.

Everyone watched the boy pedal off, chasing Darius.

"If he uses the seventh gear," said Daedalus, "we may never see him again."

"Why?" asked Miss Hastings. "What will happen?"

"I'm not sure," said Daedalus. "He'll go careening off to some other part of the universe, I think."

"Stop him! Please stop him," pleaded Gertrude Gritbun.

But no one had ever learned how to stop Anthony. Not even Colonel Crimper.

Darius, heart pounding, stood on the pedals and pumped so hard his legs ached. He veered around the next corner and narrowly missed colliding with a delivery truck. He glanced behind him. Anthony, bigger and stronger and riding Daedalus's much more powerful bicycle, was gaining on him fast. The boy was now so close that Darius could hear him panting. Anthony drew closer and closer as the two bikes screamed down the street.

Darius didn't know how much longer he could keep up this pace. The pain in his legs was almost unbearable, and the wheels on his bike were beginning to wobble a little from the speed. He looked down at the shifter. He was in fifth gear. Darius read the sign again. The warning was clear.

> CAUTION: SIXTH GEAR FOR
> EMERGENCIES ONLY.
> HOLD ON TIGHT. DON'T FLY ALONE!

Darius couldn't think of a bigger emergency than this. If Anthony caught him, he would be sent away to Crapper Academy where he'd have to live with that bully for twenty-four hours a day, along with five hundred other boys who were probably just like him. He would lose Daedalus—and Miss Hastings, after he had just found her again. A wicked laugh interrupted his thoughts.

"I've got you, you worm!" Anthony called out.

I know what you are wishing.

For once, your wish has been granted.

Darius couldn't imagine the bike going any faster, but he figured it was his only hope. "Here we go!" he screamed, and he flicked the gear shifter into sixth gear.

As soon as the sixth gear locked into place, the most amazing thing happened. The pedals seemed to give way under his feet, as if the chain had fallen off the teeth of the sprocket. He could no longer hear the solid hum of the wheels on the pavement, only a high-pitched whir.

"Oh no!" Darius cried. "Oh no!" He was sure his bike was broken. He looked back at the rear wheel and saw that the chain was still on the sprocket. He kept pedaling, faster and faster. The next time he looked back, he felt a cold thrill and his heart almost stopped. The wheels were no longer on the road. They were spinning freely two feet above the pavement. By the time Darius turned his head back to the front, he was climbing over a car stopped at an intersection. He was flying!

Twenty feet in the air!

He gained in altitude, rising to the tops of the trees and over them. The street below him got smaller and smaller.

"Yeehah!" Darius screamed. "YEEHAH! YEEHAHAH!" He tilted the handlebars to the right, and the bike made a wide banking turn, so he was leaning over, looking down at the entire town.

When Darius took off into the air, Anthony cursed and yelled. Without a thought, he shoved the gear shifter up to the sixth notch. Anthony's stomach lurched as his bike left the ground and soared over the rooftops. "Aieeeee!" he shrieked, holding onto the handlebars for dear life. His legs trembled in fear and he stopped pedaling. As soon as he did, the bike started to descend, heading toward a tree.

"Help!" Anthony screamed. Someone help me! He started to pedal again, more frantically than before. The bike angled upward, lifing just in time to brush the top leaves of the tree. A flock of blackbirds rose out of the branches like a dark cloud and surrounded him, whistling and shrieking.

"Aughh!" he said. "Get out of here, you creepy birds!" The blackbirds veered away from him and Anthony kept pedaling, heading up into the blue.

"Whoa, baby!" he shouted. "I'm flying!!"

Darius looped around and passed Anthony going the other way.

Anthony made a wide turn and followed him. "Look out, here I come!" he called out. "I'm catching you and I'm not even in seventh gear yet. Faster and higher than you!" He caught up with Darius and soared past him. Anthony seemed to have forgotten about catching Darius—now he was just showing off.

Darius coasted along, not at all interested in a race with Anthony. Here in the sky, it was strangely quiet; there was only the whir and click of the bicycle wheels. The sun shone between large puffy clouds, and for a brief moment, Darius forgot about everything else.

"I've never seen the sky so blue," he said out loud.

He looked down directly beneath him. Daedalus's yard, filled with bicycles, was a wonderful jumble of color and design, shining in the sun. It was like his father's maps, but more vibrant, more alive. It was real.

No wonder my father loved flying so much! he thought. Quite clearly, in his mind's eye, he could see his father smiling at him. And then he saw a jumble of images—Darius couldn't tell whether they were in his mind or up ahead through the clouds. First, he saw an enormous balloon, drifting through the air over a great blue ocean, with gigantic crests of waves rising and falling, stretching away to the far horizon.

Then, just as clearly, he saw and felt his father holding the bicycle for him on the street where he had grown up. His father's hand was on his shoulder, and Darius heard the *ching ching ching* of the change in his father's pocket as he ran along beside the bike. The next instant he felt himself riding down the street alone and free. The bike wobbled as he turned back, and he saw his father standing there in the middle of the street, his arms outstretched. "Come home, flyboy!" his father called. "Come back, all on your own!"

Then the sun came out from behind a cloud and shone down on Darius's face. The image he had just seen disappeared.

"Come back!" A familiar voice drifted up to him from way below. Darius looked down and once again he saw Daedalus's house. In the front yard, gathered around Colonel Crimper's car and the tumble of bikes, stood the tiny figures of Daedalus, Miss Hastings, Aunt Inga, Mrs. Gritbun, and the colonel, all looking up into the sky, shielding their eyes from the bright sun. Darius shook his head in disbelief. He must have been imagining the ocean and his father's balloon. It had seemed so real, but now here he was, on the shiny red bicycle, back over the bike shop again.

Something in Darius still wanted to go on, go faster.

To fly away.

Chasing his father.

Off into the sky.

Forever.

Like Icarus, who flew higher than anyone else had flown.

"Come back, Darius," Daedalus called again, waving and flapping his arms. "Come back! We love you!"

"We love you, Darius!" Miss Hastings cried.

When Darius heard those words, his heart lifted up in his chest. He remembered the silver wings on the chain Miss Hastings had given him. She'd been right. He *could* fly.

He stopped pedaling for a moment, coasting in midair. He looked down at the group of people beneath him.

And then Darius realized something.

Flying was exciting and beautiful. It was exactly what he had dreamed of. If he chose to, he could soar away and never have to worry about Aunt Inga or Crapper Academy ever again. But now that he was flying free, Darius realized that he didn't want to go higher or faster. He wanted to be with Daedalus and Miss Hastings. That was what he had wanted all along.

In that moment, Darius wasn't afraid of Aunt Inga or Colonel Crimper anymore.

Miss Hastings and Daedalus were calling to him, and he would fly to them.

Darius slowed his pedaling. The bike began to descend toward earth slowly, like a balloon leaking air.

Suddenly Anthony was beside him.

"Gotcha!" the older boy said. He turned his handlebars and bumped into Darius's bike—both boys wobbled in the air.

"Stop it, Anthony," said Darius. "I'm going back down."

"No you're not. This is way too much fun. Look at this!" Anthony turned the bike in a hard loop and circled around Darius. He rose in the air, then pulled the bike over in a series of somersaults, turning upside down in wild loops.

"How do you like that!" he chortled. "And I haven't even tried seventh gear yet. You won't stand a chance of beating me then."

Darius's bike didn't have a seventh gear. The sixth gear was enough for him. "I don't care," he said. "I'm not racing. Let's go back down."

"No way," said Anthony. He seemed to have completely forgotten where he was and what he was doing. "Watch me when I go into seventh gear."

Darius looked on as Anthony pushed the shifter to the last gear. The larger bike paused and hovered in the air.

"Hey, nothing's happening with this stupid gear," Anthony said. He wrenched the gear shifter back and forth.

And then, slowly at first, the bike began to shudder and quiver. It jittered and wobbled more and more in the air, like it was being shaken by a giant pair of hands.

"Hey! What's going on? Hey!" Anthony pedaled backwards, then forwards, shoving the shifter back and forth as the bike vibrated more and more violently. Darius watched from a short distance away, unsure of what to do.

"Help!" Anthony called out, "Something's wrong. Somebody help!" The shaking became so wild, so violent, that he began to lose his balance. He clung on to the handlebars as the bike bucked up and down. Then, with one giant vibration, it threw him off the seat, and he was dangling from the handlebars with his legs kicking in the air in front of the bike. The bicycle rocked and twisted as if it were trying to throw him out of the sky.

"I'm gonna fall! I'm gonna fall!" Anthony screamed. "Help. Help meeeee!" He whimpered and sobbed as his hands slipped from the handlebars and down the side of the front forks that held the front wheel. Both hands grabbed hold of the bottom of the wheel as it rocked back and forth. In a moment he would fall.

The end of Anthony.

What do you think? What would you do?

Darius didn't even think. He pedaled his bike up toward Anthony and positioned his rear fender right under Anthony's dangling legs.

"I've got you, Anthony," Darius called. "Sit on the fender. Grab my shoulders."

For once in his life, Anthony listened.

His legs slid down on either side of Darius's rear wheel, and when he was sitting on the rear fender of the red bike, he let go of the bucking, twisting bicycle. With Anthony's weight added, Darius's bike dropped suddenly in the sky. Darius pedaled hard, and the bike rose again, balancing gently in the air. He looked up at Anthony's bike, still twisting and shaking above them.

And then, there was a clear, bell-like sound, as if someone had gently tapped a beautiful crystal glass with a fork or a spoon.

Pling!

With that sound, the twisting, turning bike vanished into thin air.

"Wow," said Darius. "Did you see that?"

But Anthony was too busy sobbing behind him to notice what had happened.

"Get me down from here," the older boy wailed. "Get me down right now."

Darius pedaled slowly, and the bike began to descend. It was a long way down, and Darius began to turn the bike in slow, graceful circles. He enjoyed every moment in the air, even with Anthony whimpering behind him. Below, Darius saw Daedalus's yard and the grown-ups looking up at him.

Miss Hastings was waving her arms. "Yoo-hoo," she called. "Yoo-hoo! Here! Come back here!"

Darius circled round and round until at last the tires touched down on the pavement on the street near Daedalus's house. With all the adults watching, he coasted to a stop directly in front of them.

18
Back on Earth

Gertrude Gritbun waddled up to the bike as Darius came to a stop.

"Anthony. My Anthony! Are you all right?"

Her son practically fell off the rear fender and struggled to his feet. He wiped his face with his hands, hoping to hide his tears. Darius climbed off the bicycle, lay it on the ground, and ran to Miss Hastings.

"Miss Hastings! I thought I'd never see you again!"

"Oh my," Miss Hastings said, "How terrible that would have been!"

Darius hugged her and she hugged him back. She smelled like lemons and felt like home. As they held each other, Darius felt another pair of arms around both him and his old housekeeper. Daedalus had joined them, and they were all wrapped up together.

But their reunion was quickly disturbed. Anthony had recovered and was back to being his usual self. "You!" he said, pointing at Daedalus. "Your stupid bike almost killed me! I almost fell!"

"Hmm," said Daedalus with a bemused look on his face, "it seems to me that you owe Darius a thank-you."

"Thank him?" said Anthony, "Why should I thank him? If it wasn't for him, I never would have been on that dumb bike."

"I told you not to get on that bike," Daedalus said. "You heard me very well, but you didn't listen."

"You shouldn't have bikes like that lying around," said Gertrude Gritbun. "My son could have been hurt. Maybe we'll sue."

"That is the silliest thing I've ever heard," said Miss Hastings. "Your son doesn't listen and you blame someone else. You should be ashamed of yourselves. Daedalus tried to stop him and got pushed over for his trouble. And if it wasn't for Darius, this boy would have died. Darius saved his life. We all know it."

Gertrude Gritbun spluttered and Colonel Crimper grimaced. Aunt Inga sniffed. But no one said anything because they knew it was true.

"Whatever," mumbled Anthony. He looked at the ground and scowled.

You probably want Anthony to apologize and thank Darius. No chance.

"Miss Hastings," Darius said, "How did you get here?"

"I took a bus last night. Yesterday I was unpacking a box I took with me from your father's house. There were things from his desk I should have gone through before. You know how messy that desk was! Even those Figby and Migby people wouldn't go through everything. I couldn't bear to look at things right away. When I finally did, I found a letter in an envelope. He hadn't even bothered to address it—he must have gotten sidetracked. Here it is."

With trembling hands, Miss Hastings reached into her sweater pocket and pulled out an envelope. Everyone watched as she opened it and read.

> *To whom it may concern,*
> *In the event of my demise or disappearance, I would like my housekeeper, Miss Grace Hastings, to become the guardian of my son, Darius Frobisher. While Inga Burnslacker, his great-aunt, is his closest relative, I think it best for everyone if he stays with Miss Hastings. I know she loves him.*
> *Rudolph Frobisher*

Miss Hastings paused to gather herself, then continued. "So this morning I took a bus here. I called Daedalus from the bus station."

"I picked her up on the tandem bicycle," Daedalus said.

Miss Hastings sighed. "It was a call I should have made forty years ago."

"I knew you were here," said Darius. "I smelled the burnt toast."

"Your bike was ready," said Daedalus, "but you didn't really need it."

"It sure flew," said Darius.

"Yes, it did," Daedalus said with a grin.

Then Darius heard a hissing and spluttering. It was Aunt Inga. She was breathing heavily.

"Fine," she said. "This is just a fine kettle of fish. Why should I expect anything different? You've been nothing but a burden to me, and what do I get from it? Nothing."

"Aunt Inga—" Darius began.

"Aunt Inga!" she mimicked. "You listen to me, you—"

"No," said Darius, quite sure of himself now. "You listen to me!"

"Hold on a minute there, soldier," said Colonel Crimper.

"I am not a soldier, and I never want to be one." Darius paused, taking a deep breath. Something inside him knew what was right and true, and he had to speak. "I have some things to say." Darius had never spoken so forcefully before and his whole body was trembling.

"Aunt Inga," Darius began again. "I'm not coming back. I knew from the beginning you didn't want me to live with you. From the first time you saw me you have been mean to me. You're so wrapped up in yourself, you don't even know how mean you are! I was sad and alone, and you were never nice to me. Not even for a minute. You never even hugged me. Not one hug!"

It was very quiet. No one moved.

"And you hid Miss Hastings's letters. You lied to me! Why did you do that? Why did you lie?"

Darius glanced around at the other grown-ups. Daedalus and Miss Hastings were nodding their heads. Colonel Crimper was grimacing, as if he'd seen a creature from deep space. Then Darius looked back at his aunt. He was waiting for her to yell. But she didn't.

Instead, her mouth formed an O like a small donut, and the color drained from her angry red cheeks. She breathed in and out noisily, sounding like an air pump. Her bottom lip began to quiver. It quivered and shook until it was positively flapping up and down like the mouth of a balloon letting out all of its air.

And then Darius saw her hand go toward her eyes. She was wiping away a tear.

147

Aunt Inga was crying.

In spite of how angry he had been at Aunt Inga and how much he wanted to get away from her, Darius did feel a little sorry for her. Aunt Inga was deflating in front of him like a punctured inner tube. "No one ever understands all the hardships I have to endure," she blubbered. "Those Migby Figby people took advantage of me. I should never have let them talk me into taking in a needy little boy. I don't know what to say to children. I never understood them. And I barely have the resources to keep myself going. I knew nothing good would come of it."

Aunt Inga sniffled and snorted. She wiped her nose with the back of her hand, then wiped her hand on her dress. "I took those letters for your own good. There was no point in giving them to you so you could cry and go on about your beloved babysitter. I knew you didn't like me from the beginning. No one likes me."

Mrs. Gritbun walked over to Aunt Inga and patted her shoulder. "There, there, Ingy. I like you."

"Oh," sniffled Aunt Inga, "you just like my cookies."

"No, no, no," protested Gertrude. "I like you. I really do. Although I must admit those cookies are tasty."

"Ahem." Colonel Crimper cleared his throat. "Excuse me, ma'am. Um...uh, Darius's aunt—whatever your name is."

Aunt Inga turned and glared at the colonel.

"I'm sorry, ma'am. I no longer consider your nephew a suitable candidate for our academy. Insolence and delinquency we can fix. And we can correct a smart-aleck. But this creative stuff—disobeying direct orders, speaking up for himself, flying off on an unapproved vehicle—it has no place at Crapper. An insubordinate young man like this would disrupt all our discipline. It takes time and effort to take such behavior out of a young boy. I'm afraid it's too late for him."

"You can't fix me?" asked Darius, "You mean I'm already ruined? For life?"

"I'm afraid so, son. You're a mess."

"Hooray," said Darius. "Hooray, hooray!"

"Hooray!" chorused Daedalus and Miss Hastings.

The colonel turned to Anthony. "As for you, soldier, all I can say is I'm disappointed. This fellow isn't even a junior cadet, and he had to save you. It was a pathetic display of incompetence up there for everyone to see. Before you're ever captain of the guard, I think you'll need some seasoning. A little bathroom duty ought to help."

Anthony's shoulders slumped, and he looked as miserable as Darius had ever seen him. In spite of himself, Darius even felt a little sorry for Anthony.

"Yes, Colonel Crimper, sir," Anthony said.

The colonel grabbed Anthony by the arm and led him to his big black car.

"Anthony, honey," Gertrude Gritbun said. "Aren't you going to say good-bye? How about a good-bye kiss?"

Anthony only raised his hand and shook his head as Colonel Crimper stuffed him in the car. A sad look passed over Gertrude Gritbun's face. Now, Darius even felt a little sorry for her.

Everyone watched the car drive away.

"I'm quite tired," said Aunt Inga in a small voice. "I'm going home." She turned to leave.

"Wait for me, Ingy," said Mrs. Gritbun. "I'll walk with you."

Aunt Inga and Anthony's mother headed home. Darius was left standing with Miss Hastings and Daedalus.

"Welcome back to Earth," said Daedalus. "I'm glad you came down."

"It's so good to see you," said Miss Hastings.

"I had to come back," said Darius. "When I was up there pedaling, I kept thinking and seeing all these things in my mind. At least, I think they were in my mind. I thought I saw my dad in a balloon. And then, I thought about the time my dad taught me to ride a bicycle. He let go, and at first I was afraid. Then I was really excited when I saw I could balance on my own. But the thing I remembered most clearly was riding back to my dad. 'Come home,' he called. 'Come home, flyboy.' Up there in the sky, I knew I could fly away on my own, but I wanted to come back. To both of you."

"And that's what we want," said Miss Hastings. "Don't you think so, Daedalus?" She looked up shyly at her old friend.

"Yes, indeed." Daedalus nodded. "Yes, indeed."

"Let's go have a snack," said Miss Hastings. "I think I have some toast in the toaster."

"Okay," said Darius, "but you have to tell me about everything. You have to tell me what happened to that bike up there."

"All in good time," said Daedalus. "I will as well as I can."

"And you have to tell me what happened to you two."

"All right," said Miss Hastings, " We will. As well as we can."

"I think you'd better lock up that bike, Darius," said Daedalus. "We don't want anyone taking it for a ride and being a little surprised at what happens."

19
What Happened a Long Time Ago

Miss Hastings began. "I was working for your grandparents. I was very young."

"And very beautiful," said Daedalus. He reached across the kitchen table and squeezed Miss Hastings's hand. Darius looked at Miss Hastings. It wasn't hard to imagine her as young and beautiful.

"I met Daedalus in the park," she said, "while I was taking your father for a walk."

Then Daedalus chimed in. "It was my lunch hour. I used to take a break from my work at the physics laboratory and walk in the park. And of course, I always carried some tools with me just in case someone needed a little help with their bicycle or tricycle."

"He loved to help people fix things," Miss Hastings said.

"He still does," said Darius.

Daedalus flashed a quick smile and went on. "The first time I saw Gracie there, I knew she was someone special. She was very good with your father. He was very, very active. Even then."

"He could never sit still," said Miss Hastings.

"We fell in love," said Daedalus. "And I got to know your father. He was a wonderful boy."

"Daedalus could entertain Rudy for hours on end with his marvelous stories and handmade toys," she added. "He even built a bike for Rudy and taught him how to ride it."

"And should have stopped there," said Daedalus.

"Daedalus was quite brilliant, you know." Miss Hastings winked at Darius. "He had advanced quickly in his job at the science lab. Then one day he told me that he was working on a project of his own—a very unusual bicycle. He was searching for a way to make it fly through...um...changing something."

"Gyroscopic polarity," said Daedalus. "And incomplete entry into a seventh dimension."

"Yes, that's it," said Miss Hastings. "I never understood any of it. And no one else ever did, either. Everyone at the science lab thought he was crazy, so he worked on it in secret. He finished building his flying bicycle just about the time we were going to be married. Rudy, who was only eleven years old at the time, heard him talking about the bike, and begged to ride it. I was afraid that Daedalus was going to let him. I said 'no.' I was very protective of Rudy."

"It was your job," said Daedalus.

"Sometimes I was too protective," said Miss Hastings. "I said 'no' to so many things in those days that your father just went behind my back and rode the bike anyway."

Darius had a hard time picturing Miss Hastings being strict. She had always let him do just about anything he wanted to.

"No, it was my fault," said Daedalus. "I should have prepared him better for flying. Your father was so excited, and I was too eager to prove that my invention was a success."

"But you didn't give him permission," Miss Hastings protested. "He did it on his own."

"Still my fault," said Daedalus. "And now, look what happened. Rudy disappeared in a hot air balloon—and it's because of my bicycle."

"Don't be ridiculous," said Miss Hastings. "Rudy was always headstrong. He was going to fly whether you helped him or not. But, before, when he fell...I was angry with you."

"I am sorry—"

"But you kept the bike," interrupted Darius. "You kept my father's bike all this time."

"Yes," Daedalus said. "I just couldn't understand what had gone wrong. I've fixed a thousand other bikes, but I never fixed that one, because of what happened. I spent years trying to understand my miscalculations. I was beginning to make some progress when you showed up. I was out on my bike, trying things out."

"That's when I saw you, up in the air."

Daedalus nodded. "Yes, and then we met. I could see how bright you were right away. Then, when you told me about Gracie, everything seemed to pop into place. I fixed the all the problems. Well, almost all the problems. We do have that little mystery of the disappearing bike."

"What happened to your bike? Where did it go? I just heard a little *pling* and it was gone."

"Hmm," said Daedalus. "*Pling? Not plonk or kapow?*"

"*Pling,*" said Darius.

"I'm not quite sure," mused Daedalus. "I think it entered another dimension. So it's either in another part of the universe, or in another universe entirely. It's pretty interesting. But that bike is gone, and I can't fix it now."

"Well, you fixed things for me," said Darius. "And you've fixed things up with Miss Hastings, too. I never have understood why grown-ups talk about things from the past so much. Can't you just stop worrying about things that happened a long time ago and be together now?"

Daedalus and Miss Hastings looked at each other and smiled.

"I believe that's a good idea," said Miss Hastings.

"So do I," said Daedalus.

Daedalus and Darius and Miss Hastings talked until the sun was low in the sky. And then, after some planning, they decided Darius should spend one more night at Aunt Inga's.

"It's where your toothbrush is," said Miss Hastings.

It was already getting dark when Darius got back to Aunt Inga's house. He immediately noticed how quiet the house was, and realized that the television wasn't on. Aunt Inga was in her room with the door closed.

A plate of tuna noodle casserole was waiting for him on the kitchen table. It was a little cold, but it tasted better than cookies and soda pop.

That night, Darius pulled the mattress from the basement up the stairs and laid it out in the backyard. It was a warm, clear night, and Darius lay awake in the dark, staring at the stars flung across the sky, listening to the crickets and cicadas.

The next morning Aunt Inga got up earlier than her usual ten o'clock. She wasn't exactly nice to Darius, but not exactly mean either. Trying to be friendly, Darius sat watching television with Aunt Inga. Neither of them spoke. The show was boring, and Darius's mind wandered. Sometimes, Aunt Inga glanced at Darius and opened her mouth as if to say something, but then closed it again and went back to watching. Finally, she got up from her chair, turned off the television, and with a huge sigh, headed back to her bedroom.

Darius waited patiently. He knew visitors would be arriving soon.

Just before lunchtime, Daedalus and Miss Hastings showed up at Aunt Inga's house on the tandem bicycle. Darius showed them into the living room. He knocked on the door of Aunt Inga's room.

"Aunt Inga, someone is here to see you."

His aunt opened her bedroom door. There were bags under her eyes. She hobbled across the living room and settled herself down in her big chair. She looked horrible.

"Yes," she said, "what is it?"

"Aunt Inga," said Darius, "Miss Hastings and Daedalus are planning to get married soon." He paused, watching his aunt's face. "They've invited me to come and live with them, like they were my grandparents."

Darius couldn't read the expression on Aunt Inga's face. It might have been a smile. Or maybe a frown.

"That's nice," she said. She almost sounded like she meant it.

"The letter from my dad that Miss Hastings found means that you don't have to worry about taking care of me anymore. But you are my aunt, and I thought...I mean, is it okay with you if I go?"

Aunt Inga didn't say anything at first. She just looked at the floor.

Darius was jumping up and down inside, but he didn't speak.

"Well, I don't know," Aunt Inga began. "I suppose it might be possible..."

Before Darius had a chance to say anything, Miss Hastings spoke up. "I know you must have gotten used to having someone around."

"Well, not exactly, but sort of," Aunt Inga said, without looking up.

"I'm sure Mrs. Gritbun will be happy to come by for a chat every day," Miss Hastings continued. "With Anthony away at school, she'll need lots of company. I think you two might go a long way toward cheering each other up."

Aunt Inga still looked unconvinced. And then Darius offered something he had not planned to offer. "I'd come visit you, too, Aunt Inga," he said. "Twice a week. At least that."

She gave Darius a surprised look. "You would visit me?" she asked.

"If you want," said Darius.

"A little visit once in a while might be nice," Aunt Inga said. "But you must promise not to come before ten o'clock."

"I promise."

"And no books."

"No ma'am."

"And certainly no bicycles."

"No bicycles."

"Well," his aunt said, "I suppose this arrangement might work."

Darius's heart soared. He stood up and jumped in the air. "Yippee!" he yelled. "Yippee, yippee! Thank you, thank you, Aunt Inga." Before he realized what he was doing, he wrapped his arms around his aunt and gave her a big hug.

"Here now," spluttered Aunt Inga. "You'll mess up my dress. I knew this would happen. I give you an inch and you take a mile."

She pulled away from Darius, but he could see the tiniest trace of a smile on the corners of her mouth. "Be sure that you clean up all that clutter you left in the basement before you go," she said.

"Thank you, ma'am," said Daedalus. "We'll take very good care of Darius."

"Good-bye," said Miss Hastings.

"Well, what do you know," said Aunt Inga. "I never thought this would happen."

20
Time Will Tell

Darius moved in with Daedalus and Miss Hastings. It took quite a bit of work to make room for everyone—they spent several days rearranging books and bicycle parts. Two months later, Darius's two best friends were married in their backyard, amid the piles of bicycles.

Darius visited his aunt twice a week, sometimes more, and the Panforths occasionally invited Aunt Inga and Mrs. Gritbun over for dinner.

Over the months that followed, Aunt Inga and Darius actually became friends of a sort. I never would have believed that could have happened. Maybe you wouldn't have either. A change of heart is one of the greatest of miracles. And while it is rare, it can happen almost anywhere, to almost anyone.

Darius and Daedalus continued repairing bikes, and soon they were doing a booming business. The yard was filled with even more parts of even more bicycles. They didn't make much money, because most of their customers were children. Neither of them cared.

After some discussion between them, Darius and Daedalus decided that the flying bicycles needed more thought.

"I'm onto something," said Daedalus, "but it seems a little dangerous to experiment with a seventh dimension when human beings are involved."

"I'll try it!" said Darius.

"Oh no, you won't!" said Daedalus. "Miss Hastings would murder me."

Darius laughed at the thought of Miss Hastings murdering anyone.

And what of Darius's father, Rudy?

You are probably hoping that one day they will get a letter from him.

Or that he will show up on the doorstep, dressed in sealskins, with stories about life in Greenland.

Or that Darius, Daedalus, and Miss Hastings will ride off on their bikes and find him.

No, I'm sorry to say that Rudy Frobisher will not come back in this book. But stories go on, and there is more to this story than I have told you. Only time will tell.

For now, I'll just say that Darius was happier than he had been for a long time. Sometimes at night, he and Daedalus would sit on the roof of the house and look at the stars. Daedalus would tell stories of the Greek gods and mortals, pointing out the different constellations: Cassiopeia, Orion, Heracles, and all the others that filled the sky with marvelous tales.

One night they saw a bright object passing overhead, traveling across the sky.

"A satellite," Daedalus said.

"Maybe," Darius responded. "Or maybe it's your bicycle!"

"Could be," said Daedalus.

"Or maybe it's my dad!"

"Hmm," Daedalus said, "maybe. It should be."

"Why should it be?" asked Darius.

"Because," said Daedalus, "it makes such a wonderful story— Rudy, the man in the fabulous flying balloon. As wonderful a story as any Greek myth."

"It's sad, though," said Darius.

"Sad and happy. Both are possible," said Daedalus. "Sometimes at the same time."

Darius nodded. "Do you smell something burning, Daedalus?"

"Yes," said Daedalus, "it's time to go inside. I think the toast is ready."

Bill Harley—an accomplished storyteller, musician, and writer— has been writing and performing for kids and families for more than twenty years. He has performed at the presti-gious National Storytelling Festival and at dozens of regional festivals and is a regular commentator on NPR's "All Things Considered." He is the recipient of Parents Choice and ALA awards and has twice been nominated for a Grammy Award.

The idea for the book came to Harley one morning after he wrote a paragraph describing a boy's bike taking off unexpectedly into the air. How did that happen? he wondered. He had to write THE AMAZING FLIGHT OF DARIUS FROBISHER to find out.